CONTENTS

i	INTRODUCTION
1	PREPARING FOR PESACH
14	KADESH
21	URCHATZ
22	KARPAS
23	YACHATZ
26	MAGGID
65	RACHTZAH
68	MOTZI MATZAH
69	MAROR
70	KORECH
72	SHULCHAN ORECH
74	TZAFUN
76	BARECH
84	HALLEL
96	NIRTZAH
116	PHOEBE'S JINGLES
137	EPISODE GUIDE

INTRODUCTION

As Passover approaches, Monica goes into full blown cleaning-mode, wiping the apartment of all the chametz. While she is cleaning her apartment, she discovers an old Passover cookbook which belonged to her grandmother. She decides to do what she loves most: cooking and hosting a Seder for her friends.

Chandler recites the Ma Nishtanah, "Can this night BE any more different than all the other nights?"

As the Seder unfolds, Joey's stomach rumbles loudly while he turns the pages to count down towards Shulchan Orech. He decides to fill up on Wine, Karpas, and Maror in the meantime exclaiming "Wine, good. Potatoes, good. Bitter herbs, GOOD."

While the rest of the gang is busy finding a hiding spot for the Afikoman, Ross is hiding his sandwich.

After the recitation of Dayenu, Rachel remarks, "It's not that common, it doesn't happen to every nation, and it is a big deal!"

Phoebe volunteers to open the door for Elijah the Prophet as she is familiar with communicating with spirits.

Relive your favorite FRIENDS scenes through the lens of the Pesach Haggadah.

_{All direct quotes or scenes begin with an episode reference above. If the scene includes a picture, the picture will not be referenced again. Any indirect text, or photo which does not follow a scene will be referenced with a number which can be found in the back of the Haggadah under "Episode Guide."}

_{This book contains the holy name of God, and should be treated with the utmost care and respect.}

PREPARING FOR PESACH

Cleaning for Pesach

S4E6: The One With the Dirty Girl
Ross: You know how you throw your jacket on a chair at the end of the day? Well, like that, only instead of a chair, it's a pile of garbage. And instead of a jacket, it's a pile of garbage! And instead of the end of the day, it's the end of time, and garbage is ALL that has survived!

The house is not just clean, it's "Monica Clean"[1]

S6E7: The One Where Phoebe Runs
(Chandler finished unpacking his boxes in Monica's apartment and decides to clean the apartment for her.)
Ross: What are you doing?
Chandler: What does it look like? I am cleaning.
Ross: Did you get Monica's authorization to move all of her stuff?
Chandler: Authorization? I don't need that, I'm going to put everything back.
Ross: Put it back exactly where you found it?
Chandler: Yes, I'm going to put it back 'exactly' where I found it.
Ross: K, first of all, that attitude is not helping.
Chandler: She's not gonna care if I put her stuff back in the same stupid place.
Ross: Uh, hello, did you just meet Monica?
Chandler: She is going to recognize that I did a nice thing, and, and appreciate it.
Ross: Huh, no actually, this is going to work out well, because when you have to move back in with Joey, Joey's hot new roommate can come live with me!
Chandler: I see, I see, y-y-you're trying to freak me out.
Ross: Look Chandler, Monica is really weird about this kind of stuff. Believe me, I lived with her for sixteen years, she is going to freak out. Oh my gosh, she is going to sit on you.
Chandler: No she's not, ok I'll prove it to you. I'll call her right now. (Calls Monica on the phone) Hey Mon, how's it going?
Monica: Terrible. If I want something done right, I have to do it myself. Other people just wreck stuff! I really think I might kill someone tonight!
Chandler: Oh c'mon, c'mon, it can't be that bad!
Monica: It's worse! The only thing that's getting me through is knowing that I'm going to be seeing you soon. I think I might even try to get out of here early.
Chandler: No, no! No no no no no! It sounds like they really need you down there!
Monica: Well, are you just hanging out with Ross?
Chandler: It's all good! Ok, bye Mon! I love you! (Hangs up and turns to Ross) She's going to kill me!
Ross: You know the phone was facing the other way....and that goes back up there.

Bedikas Chametz

S6E18: The One Where Ross Dates a Student
[Over at Hotel Monica, Phoebe is on the bed playing her guitar as Monica enters.]
Monica: Hey! How's it goin'?
Phoebe: Well, not much has changed in the last five minutes.
Monica: Yes it has! I made cookies!
Phoebe: Oh that's all right. I'm still full from your homemade potato chips.
Monica: But you should eat them now because they're hot from the oven.
Phoebe: Okay. (Reaches for one.)
Monica: (pulling the plate back) Oh-ho! But not in here! Can't eat 'em in bed, remember? No crummies!
Phoebe: (gritting her teeth) Okay, I'll be out in a second.
Monica: Okay!
(Monica leaves and Phoebe closes the door behind her and tries to lock it.)
Monica: (opening the door) What are you doing?
Phoebe: That doesn't lock, does it?

Can't eat them in bed, remember? No crummies.

S2E21: The One With the Bullies
Rachel: Ok, doggie get the- aahhh. Ok go get the sandwich, get the sandwich doggie. (dog ignores the sandwich) Good doggie get the sandwich, get the...ok, Joey, the dog will lick himself but he will not touch your sandwich, what does that tell you?
Joey: Well if he's not gonna eat it, I will.

Blessed are You, our God, Ruler of the world, who sanctifies us with mitzvot and calls upon us to remove chametz.

בָּרוּךְ אַתָּה, יְיָ אֱלֹהֵינוּ, מֶלֶךְ הָעוֹלָם אֲשֶׁר קִדְּשָׁנוּ בְּמִצְוֹתָיו, וְצִוָּנוּ עַל בִּעוּר חָמֵץ.

Any leaven that is in my possession, that I have not seen or not removed, shall be unclaimed and considered as the dust of the earth.

כָּל־חֲמִירָא וַחֲמִיעָא דְּאִכָּא בִרְשׁוּתִי דְּלָא חֲמִתֵּהּ וּדְלָא בַעַרְתֵּהּ לִבְטִיל וְלֶהֱוֵי כְּעַפְרָא דְאַרְעָא.

Ohh, the-the Foster puppets![3]

Biur Chametz

Make sure to burn your Chametz responsibly.

Who to Invite
S2E22: *The One With the Two Parties*

Ross: I talked to Rachel's sisters, neither of them can come.
Monica: Okay, so I still have to invite Dylan and Emma and Shannon Cooper.
Joey: Whoa, whoa, whoa, no Shannon Cooper
Phoebe: Why not her?
Joey: Because she….she steals stuff…
Chandler: Or maybe she doesn't steal stuff and Joey just slept with her and never called her back….

………………………………………………………………………………

(Rachel comes in complaining about her parents behavior at her sisters graduation from college)
Rachel: They got into a huge fight in middle of the commencement address, Bishop Tutu actually had to stop and shush them! (walks off)
Phoebe: Ok, so how about we don't invite her parents?
Monica: Well, how about just her mom?
Chandler: Why her mom?
Monica: Because I already invited her.
Phoebe: Oh, did you ask Stacy Roth?
Joey: Uh, can't invite her. (Everyone looks at Joey with bewilderment) She also steals…

Guest list
1. ~~Shannon Cooper~~
2. Mrs. Green ✓
3. ~~Stacy Roth~~

Preparing the Seder

S8E21: The One with the Cooking Class
Monica: Hey Joey, come taste this.
Joey: What is it?
Monica: Remember that guy that gave me a bad review? Well... [Feeds him a spoonful of what she's cooking] I'm getting my revenge!
Joey: You cooked him?

You heard the woman! **PEEL! CHOP! DEVIL!** [5]

S9E20: The One With the Soap Opera Party
Rachel: Okay, that would be two cups of tarragon, one pound of baking soda and one red onion?
Monica: What the hell are you cooking?

S10E16: The One with Rachel's Going Away Party
Monica: Okay, we're gonna start in the kitchen. Plates get put into plate protectors and stacked ten to a box. The silverware gets bundled in rubber bands and then bubble wrapped. Got it?
Joey: Yeah.
Monica: Good. Now I need you to be careful and efficient. And remember, if I'm harsh with you, it is only because you're doing it wrong. [6]

Monica, in her finest wardrobe, planning the menu.

S2E22: The One With the Two Parties

Monica: So I'll get candles and my mom's lace tablecloth….since I want it to be special, I thought I'd poach a salmon.

THE MENU

- Ross's Moist Maker Sandwich[7].
- Monica's:
    - Individual Sweet Potato Stuffed Pumpkin[8].
    - Strawberry Jam "What's the opposite of man? Jam![9]
    - 3 types of potatoes: peas and onions, lumpy mashed potatoes, potato tots[10].
    - Mockolate[11].
- Phoebe's Grandmothers' Nestle Toll House cookies[12].
- Rachel's Traditional English Trifle[13].
    - Ladyfingers
    - Jam
    - Custard
    - Raspberries
    - More ladyfingers
    - Beef sauteed with peas and onions
    - Custard
    - Bananas
    - Whipped cream on top
- Cheesecake from Mama's Little Bakery, Chicago, Illinois[14].

Seating Arrangements

Make sure to 'reserve' yourself a good seat.

Seder Plate

Starting the Seder

S3E2: The One Where No One is Ready

Ross: It starts at 8, we can't be late!

What to Wear

Alright, fine I'll be political.[22]

I'm sorry, we don't have your sheep.[23]

Could I BE wearing any more clothes?[24]

It is tradition for each person to have a pillow so they can recline comfortably.

S1E2: The One With the Sonogram
(Monica fluffing a pillow)
Phoebe: She's already fluffed that pillow. Monica, you know you already fluffed-
(Monica gives Phoebe death stare)
Phoebe: But it's fine!
Monica: Look I'm sorry guys, I just don't want to give them any more ammunition than they already have.
Chandler: Yes, and we all know how cruel a parent can be about the flatness OF a child's pillow.

KADESH

We pour the first cup. The matzot are covered.

מוזגים כוס ראשון. המצות מכוסות.

Make Kiddush

On Shabbat, begin here:

And there was evening and there was morning, the sixth day. And the heaven and the earth were finished, and all their host. And on the seventh day God finished His work which He had done; and He rested on the seventh day from all His work which He had done. And God blessed the seventh day, and sanctified it; because He rested on it from all of His work which God created in doing.

On weekdays, begin here:

Blessed are You, Lord our God, King of the universe, who creates the fruit of the vine.

קַדֵּשׁ

בְּשַׁבָּת מַתְחִילִין:

וַיְהִי עֶרֶב וַיְהִי בֹקֶר יוֹם הַשִּׁשִּׁי. וַיְכֻלּוּ הַשָּׁמַיִם וְהָאָרֶץ וְכָל־צְבָאָם. וַיְכַל אֱלֹהִים בַּיּוֹם הַשְּׁבִיעִי מְלַאכְתּוֹ אֲשֶׁר עָשָׂה וַיִּשְׁבֹּת בַּיּוֹם הַשְּׁבִיעִי מִכָּל מְלַאכְתּוֹ אֲשֶׁר עָשָׂה. וַיְבָרֶךְ אֱלֹהִים אֶת יוֹם הַשְּׁבִיעִי וַיְקַדֵּשׁ אֹתוֹ כִּי בוֹ שָׁבַת מִכָּל־מְלַאכְתּוֹ אֲשֶׁר בָּרָא אֱלֹהִים לַעֲשׂוֹת.

בחול מתחילין:

סַבְרִי מָרָנָן וְרַבָּנָן וְרַבּוֹתַי. בָּרוּךְ אַתָּה ה', אֱלֹהֵינוּ מֶלֶךְ הָעוֹלָם בּוֹרֵא פְּרִי הַגָּפֶן.

Blessed are You, Lord our God, King of the universe, who has chosen us from all peoples and has raised us above all tongues and has sanctified us with His commandments. And You have given us, Lord our God, **with love** [Sabbaths for rest], appointed times for happiness, holidays and special times for joy, [this Sabbath day, and] this Festival of matzot, our season of freedom *[in love]* a holy convocation in memory of the Exodus from Egypt. For You have chosen us and sanctified us above all peoples. In Your gracious **love**, You granted us Your [holy Sabbath, and] special times for happiness and joy. Blessed are You, O Lord, who sanctifies [the Sabbath,] Israel, and the appointed times.

On Saturday night add the following two paragraphs:

Blessed are You, Lord our God, King of the universe, who creates the light of the fire. Blessed are You, Lord our God, King of the universe, who distinguishes between the holy and the mundane,

בָּרוּךְ אַתָּה ה׳, אֱלֹהֵינוּ מֶלֶךְ הָעוֹלָם אֲשֶׁר בָּחַר בָּנוּ מִכָּל־עָם וְרוֹמְמָנוּ מִכָּל־לָשׁוֹן וְקִדְּשָׁנוּ בְּמִצְוֹתָיו. וַתִּתֶּן לָנוּ ה׳ אֱלֹהֵינוּ בְּאַהֲבָה (לשבת: שַׁבָּתוֹת לִמְנוּחָה וּ) מוֹעֲדִים לְשִׂמְחָה, חַגִּים וּזְמַנִּים לְשָׂשׂוֹן, (לשבת: אֶת יוֹם הַשַּׁבָּת הַזֶּה וְ) אֶת יוֹם חַג הַמַּצּוֹת הַזֶּה זְמַן חֵרוּתֵנוּ, (לשבת: בְּאַהֲבָה) מִקְרָא קֹדֶשׁ זֵכֶר לִיצִיאַת מִצְרָיִם. כִּי בָנוּ בָחַרְתָּ וְאוֹתָנוּ קִדַּשְׁתָּ מִכָּל הָעַמִּים, (לשבת: וְשַׁבָּת) וּמוֹעֲדֵי קָדְשֶׁךָ (לשבת: בְּאַהֲבָה וּבְרָצוֹן) בְּשִׂמְחָה וּבְשָׂשׂוֹן הִנְחַלְתָּנוּ. בָּרוּךְ אַתָּה ה׳, מְקַדֵּשׁ (לשבת: הַשַּׁבָּת וְ) יִשְׂרָאֵל וְהַזְּמַנִּים.

במוצאי שבת מוסיפים:

בָּרוּךְ אַתָּה ה׳, אֱלֹהֵינוּ מֶלֶךְ הָעוֹלָם, בּוֹרֵא מְאוֹרֵי הָאֵשׁ. בָּרוּךְ אַתָּה ה׳, אֱלֹהֵינוּ מֶלֶךְ הָעוֹלָם הַמַּבְדִּיל בֵּין קֹדֶשׁ לְחֹל,

between light and darkness, between Israel and the nations, between the seventh day and the six working days. You have distinguished between the holiness of the Sabbath and the holiness of the Festival, and You have sanctified the seventh day above the six working days. You have distinguished and sanctified Your people Israel with Your holiness.

Blessed are You, O Lord, who distinguishes between the holy and the holy.

Blessed are You, Lord our God, King of the universe, who has granted us life and sustenance and permitted us to reach this season.

Drink while reclining to the left and do not recite a blessing after drinking.

בֵּין אוֹר לְחֹשֶׁךְ, בֵּין יִשְׂרָאֵל לָעַמִּים, בֵּין יוֹם הַשְּׁבִיעִי לְשֵׁשֶׁת יְמֵי הַמַּעֲשֶׂה. בֵּין קְדֻשַּׁת שַׁבָּת לִקְדֻשַּׁת יוֹם טוֹב הִבְדַּלְתָּ, וְאֶת־יוֹם הַשְּׁבִיעִי מִשֵּׁשֶׁת יְמֵי הַמַּעֲשֶׂה קִדַּשְׁתָּ. הִבְדַּלְתָּ וְקִדַּשְׁתָּ אֶת־עַמְּךָ יִשְׂרָאֵל בִּקְדֻשָּׁתֶךָ.

בָּרוּךְ אַתָּה ה׳, הַמַּבְדִּיל בֵּין קֹדֶשׁ לְקֹדֶשׁ.

בָּרוּךְ אַתָּה ה׳, אֱלֹהֵינוּ מֶלֶךְ הָעוֹלָם, שֶׁהֶחֱיָנוּ וְקִיְּמָנוּ וְהִגִּיעָנוּ לַזְּמַן הַזֶּה.

שותה בהסיבת שמאל ואינו מברך ברכה אחרונה.

S5E12: The One With Chandler's Work Laugh
Doug (Chandlers' Boss): C'mon Honey, let's go drink our body weight, eh?

S7E16: The One With the Truth About London

We are gathered here today on this joyous occasion to celebrate the special love that Monica and Chandler share.

It is a love based of giving and receiving as well as having and sharing. And the love that they give and have is shared and received.

And through this having and giving and sharing and receiving, we too can share and love and have...and receive.

When I think of the love that these two givers and receivers share, I cannot help but envy the lifetime ahead of having and loving and giving...

S6E6: *The One on the Last Night*
Joey is upset that he's out $500 and his foosball table on the last night of being roommates with Chandler, before Chandler moves in with Monica. Chandler tries to think of ways for Joey to 'earn' some money, and invents a game called cups.
Chandler: What do you got?
Joey: A four and a nine.
Chandler: You're kidding right? That's a full cup!
Joey: Man, I am good at cups!

The Four Cups

This game depends only on luck and the player who has a combination of cards with the highest rate wins. However, the card rate in this game is reversed i.e. the lower the card the higher the rate.

Intro
Shuffle the cards. Give each player 2 cards and put the rest of the deck down. Players show cards at the same time. Person with highest rate wins. Put away used cards. Repeat step 2 - 5 until all cards are used and the player with most wins/round wins.

Cups Game Rules:
Any combination with the 2 of clubs beats all the other combinations
If players have equally high combinations, then they are to battle with one card only (instead of the usual 2 cards)

The Sitting Down Bonus
The sitting-down bonus is when a player wins 3 times in a row he/she is given 3 cards (instead of the usual two) and is allowed to make the best combination possible. Then the 3rd card not used, could be used in the next round only and in this round the player must give the extra card away.

The Saucer Cup
The Saucer Card is an Ace and only when combined with 2 of clubs, 3, 4, 6 or 9 is it a high rate combination. When an Ace is combined with other cards then the rate of the combination is lower than the lowest combination possible (King & King).

Have fun!

S1E1: The One Where Monica Gets a New Roommate
(Buzzer rings, chandler goes to answer)
Chandler (on the intercom): Please don't do that again, it's a horrible sound.
From the intercom: Ah, it's uh it's Paul.
Monica: Buzz him in!
Joey: Who's Paul?
Ross: Paul, the wine guy, Paul?
Monica: Maybe-
Joey: Wait a minute you're "not a real date" tonight is Paul, the wine guy?
Ross: He finally asked you out?!
Monica: YES!
Chandler: Oh, this is a "Dear Diary" moment.
....

Monica: Everybody, this is Paul
All: Hey! Paul! Hi! The Wine Guy! Hey!
Chandler: I'm sorry, I didn't catch your name. Paul, was it?

URCHATZ

And Wash

Wash your hands but do not say the blessing "on the washing of the hands."

וּרְחַץ

נוטלים את הידים ואין מברכים "עַל נְטִילַת יָדַיִם"

S7E8: The One Where Chandler Doesn't Like Dogs
Phoebe: Where's Chandler?
Chandler (coming out of the bathroom): Here I am.
Phoebe: Wash your hands!
Chandler (looking down at his hands): How did you know??

WASH YOUR HANDS! (without a bracha)

KARPAS

Greens

כַּרְפַּס

Take from the greens less than a kazayit - so that you will not need to say the blessing after eating it; dip it into the salt water; say the blessing "who creates the fruit of the earth;" and have in mind that this blessing will also be for the bitter herbs.
Eat without reclining.

לוקח מן הכרפס פחות מכזית – כדי שלא יתחייב בברכה אחרונה – טובל במי מלח, מברך "בורא פרי האדמה", ומכווין לפטור בברכה גם את המרור. אוכל בלא הסבה.

Blessed are you, Lord our God, King of the universe, who creates the fruit of the earth.

בָּרוּךְ אַתָּה ה', אֱלֹהֵינוּ מֶלֶךְ הָעוֹלָם, בּוֹרֵא פְּרִי הָאֲדָמָה.

Saltwater

S1E20: The One With the Evil Orthodontist

Chandler: I cannot believe you would say that...I would much rather be Mr. Peanut than Mr. Salty.
Joey: No way! Mr. Salty is a sailor, alright, he's gotta be, like, the toughest snack there is!
Ross: I don't know, you don't wanna mess with corn nuts, they're crazay!

Well, I'm a potato or a...spud.[25]

YACHATZ

Break

Split the middle matzah in two, and conceal the larger piece to use it for the afikoman.

יַחַץ

חותך את המצה האמצעית לשתים, ומצפין את הנתח הגדול לאפיקומן

WE WERE ON A BREAK!²⁶

S1E9: The One Where Underdog Gets Away

Chandler: Shall I carve?
Rachel: By all means.
Chandler: Ok, who wants light cheese, and who wants dark cheese?
Ross: I don't even wanna know about the dark cheese.
Monica: (holding sandwich) Does anybody wanna split this with me?
Joey: Oh, I will.
Phoebe: Ooh, you guys have to make a wish.
Monica: Make a wish?
Phoebe: Come on, you know, Thanksgiving. (makes breaking motion) Ooh, you got the bigger half. What'd you wish for?
Joey: The bigger half.

S7E11: The One With All the Cheesecakes

Chandler catches Rachel eating the cheesecake without him.

Rachel: You think I trust you with it?! No! We're gonna split it! You take half and I take half!

Chandler: Well that's not fair, you've already had some!

Rachel: What? Oh, well then y'know what? I think Monica would be very interested to know that you called her cheesecake dry and mealy.

Chandler: What do we use to split it?

Rachel: Okay! (Grabs a knife and cuts it in half.) All right, pick a half.

Chandler: (examining the cake) Okay well, this side looks bigger. Uh… There's more crust on this side. Y'know? So, maybe if I measured…

Rachel: Oh for God sake just pick a piece!

Chandler: All right, I'll pick that one. (Points.)

Rachel: That's also the smaller piece. (Puts the piece onto a plate.) Okay, there you go. Enjoy your half my friend, but that is it. No sharing. No switching, and don't come crying to me if you eat your piece too fast.

(She backs out the door, turns around to return to her place, stumbles and drops the cheesecake on the floor.)

Chandler: (gloatingly and holding his piece) Ohhh!

Rachel: Okay, you gotta give me some of your piece.

Chandler: Oh-ho-ho-ho-no! No! No switching! No sharing, and don't come crying to me! Ha-ha-ha! I may just sit here and have my cake all day! Just sit here in the hallway and eat my…

(Rachel knocks the plate from his hand and it falls on the floor.)

MAGGID

S10E4: The One With the Cake
Rachel: So, Joey, what are you gonna do for us?
Joey: I will be doing a dramatic reading of one of Emma's books.

The Recitation
[of the exodus story]

מגיד

The leader uncovers the matzot, raises the Seder plate, and says out loud:

מגלה את המצות, מגביה את הקערה ואומר בקול רם:

This is the bread of destitution that our ancestors ate in the land of Egypt. Anyone who is famished should come and eat, anyone who is in need should come and partake of the Pesach sacrifice. Now we are here, next year we will be in the land of Israel; this year we are slaves, next year we will be free people.

הָא לַחְמָא עַנְיָא דִּי אֲכָלוּ אַבְהָתָנָא בְּאַרְעָא דְמִצְרָיִם. כָּל דִּכְפִין יֵיתֵי וְיֵיכֹל, כָּל דִּצְרִיךְ יֵיתֵי וְיִפְסַח. הָשַׁתָּא הָכָא, לְשָׁנָה הַבָּאָה בְּאַרְעָא דְיִשְׂרָאֵל. הָשַׁתָּא עַבְדֵי, לְשָׁנָה הַבָּאָה בְּנֵי חוֹרִין.

"Anyone who is famished should come and eat."

We can truly learn this lesson from Monica, who's house is always open to all and she's always whipping up something yummy to eat.

....

But not from Joey.

Four Questions

מה נשתנה

The leader removes the plate from the table.
We pour a second cup of wine.
The son then asks:

מסיר את הקערה מעל השולחן. מוזגין כוס שני. הבן שואל:

What differentiates this night from all [other] nights?
On all [other] nights we eat chamets and matzah; this night, only matzah?
On all [other] nights we eat other vegetables; tonight (only) marror.
On all [other] nights, we don't dip [our food], even one time; tonight [we dip it] twice.
On [all] other nights, we eat either sitting or reclining; tonight we all recline.

מַה נִּשְׁתַּנָּה הַלַּיְלָה הַזֶּה מִכָּל הַלֵּילוֹת?
שֶׁבְּכָל הַלֵּילוֹת אָנוּ אוֹכְלִין חָמֵץ וּמַצָּה, הַלַּיְלָה הַזֶּה – כֻּלּוֹ מַצָּה.
שֶׁבְּכָל הַלֵּילוֹת אָנוּ אוֹכְלִין שְׁאָר יְרָקוֹת – הַלַּיְלָה הַזֶּה (כֻּלּוֹ) מָרוֹר.
שֶׁבְּכָל הַלֵּילוֹת אֵין אָנוּ מַטְבִּילִין אֲפִילוּ פַּעַם אֶחָת – הַלַּיְלָה הַזֶּה שְׁתֵּי פְעָמִים.
שֶׁבְּכָל הַלֵּילוֹת אָנוּ אוֹכְלִין בֵּין יוֹשְׁבִין וּבֵין מְסֻבִּין – הַלַּיְלָה הַזֶּה כֻּלָּנוּ מְסֻבִּין.

I mean, enough of the silliness![28]

S6E1: The One After Vegas
[In Phoebe's cab, Phoebe and Joey are driving back. Phoebe is driving while Joey is sleeping.]
Phoebe: Okay, you have 19 questions left. Use them wisely. (Joey groans.) Come on Joey! You can't win if you don't ask any (sees that he's asleep) QUESTIONS!!!

QUESTION 1

S2E22: The One with the Two Parties

Ross: Question, why do we always have to have parties where you poach things?

Monica: You want to be in charge of the food committee?

QUESTION 2

Ross: Question two - why do we always have to have parties with committees?

Joey: Ya, why can't we just get some pizzas and some beers and have fun?

Phoebe: Ya, I agree, you know, I think fancy parties are only fun if you're fancy on the inside, and I'm just not sure we are.

Monica: Alright, you guys don't want it to be special? Fine. You can throw any kind of party you want.

S1E9: The One Where Underdog Gets Away
Joey: Hey Monica, I got a question, I don't see any tater tots.
Monica: That's not a question.
Joey: Well my mom always makes them. It's like a tradition! You get a little piece of turkey on your fork, a little cranberry sauce, and a TOT!
Monica: All right fine, tonight's potatoes will be both mashed, with lumps, and in the form of tots.

QUESTION 3

Why do we lean while sitting?
S3E2: The One Where No One is Ready
Chandler: Alright, fine, you know what? We'll both sit in the chair.
Joey: Fine with me.
Chandler: I am so comfortable.
Joey: Me too, in fact, I think I might be a little too comfortable.
Chandler: Aaahh...fine, I'm going, but when I get back it's Chair City! And I'm the guy who's...sitting in a chair!

QUESTION 4

Passover is the night of many questions
S5E9: The One With Ross's Sandwich
Professor: What do you think? Uh, you in the blue shirt.
Phoebe: I think that, um, yours is a question with many possible answers.
Professor: Would you care to venture one?
Phoebe: Would YOU care to venture one?
Professor: Are you just repeating what I'm saying?
Phoebe: Are *you* just repeating what *I'm* saying?
Professor: Alright, let's move on.

We were slaves in Egypt

He puts the plate back on the table. The matzot should be uncovered during the saying of the Haggadah.

We were slaves to Pharaoh in the land of Egypt. And the Lord, our God, took us out from there with a strong hand and an outstretched forearm. And if the Holy One, blessed be He, had not taken our ancestors from Egypt, behold we and our children and our children's children would [all] be enslaved to Pharaoh in Egypt. And even if we were all sages, all discerning, all elders, all knowledgeable about the Torah, it would be a commandment upon us to tell the story of the exodus from Egypt. And anyone who adds [and spends extra time] in telling the story of the exodus from Egypt, behold he is praiseworthy.

It happened once [on Pesach] that Rabbi Eliezer, Rabbi Yehoshua, Rabbi Elazar ben Azariah, Rabbi Akiva and Rabbi Tarfon were reclining in Bnei Brak and were telling the story of the exodus from Egypt that whole night, until their students came and said to them, "The time of [reciting] the morning Shema has arrived."

עבדים היינו

מחזיר את הקערה אל השולחן. המצות תהיינה מגלות בשעת אמירת ההגדה.

עֲבָדִים הָיִינוּ לְפַרְעֹה בְּמִצְרָיִם, וַיּוֹצִיאֵנוּ ה' אֱלֹהֵינוּ מִשָּׁם בְּיָד חֲזָקָה וּבִזְרֹעַ נְטוּיָה. וְאִלּוּ לֹא הוֹצִיא הַקָּדוֹשׁ בָּרוּךְ הוּא אֶת אֲבוֹתֵינוּ מִמִּצְרַיִם, הֲרֵי אָנוּ וּבָנֵינוּ וּבְנֵי בָנֵינוּ מְשֻׁעְבָּדִים הָיִינוּ לְפַרְעֹה בְּמִצְרָיִם. וַאֲפִילוּ כֻּלָּנוּ חֲכָמִים כֻּלָּנוּ נְבוֹנִים כֻּלָּנוּ זְקֵנִים כֻּלָּנוּ יוֹדְעִים אֶת הַתּוֹרָה מִצְוָה עָלֵינוּ לְסַפֵּר בִּיצִיאַת מִצְרָיִם. וְכָל הַמַּרְבֶּה לְסַפֵּר בִּיצִיאַת מִצְרַיִם הֲרֵי זֶה מְשֻׁבָּח.

מַעֲשֶׂה בְּרַבִּי אֱלִיעֶזֶר וְרַבִּי יְהוֹשֻׁעַ וְרַבִּי אֶלְעָזָר בֶּן־עֲזַרְיָה וְרַבִּי עֲקִיבָא וְרַבִּי טַרְפוֹן שֶׁהָיוּ מְסֻבִּין בִּבְנֵי־בְרַק וְהָיוּ מְסַפְּרִים בִּיצִיאַת מִצְרַיִם כָּל־אוֹתוֹ הַלַּיְלָה, עַד שֶׁבָּאוּ תַלְמִידֵיהֶם וְאָמְרוּ לָהֶם רַבּוֹתֵינוּ הִגִּיעַ זְמַן קְרִיאַת שְׁמַע שֶׁל שַׁחֲרִית.

Rabbi Elazar ben Azariah said, "Behold I am like a man of seventy years and I have not merited [to understand why] the exodus from Egypt should be said at night until Ben Zoma explicated it, as it is stated, 'In order that you remember the day of your going out from the land of Egypt all the days of your life;' 'the days of your life' [indicates that the remembrance be invoked during] the days, 'all the days of your life' [indicates that the remembrance be invoked also during] the nights." But the Sages say, "'the days of your life' [indicates that the remembrance be invoked in] this world, 'all the days of your life' [indicates that the remembrance be invoked also] in the days of the Messiah."

אָמַר רַבִּי אֶלְעָזָר בֶּן־עֲזַרְיָה הֲרֵי אֲנִי כְּבֶן שִׁבְעִים שָׁנָה וְלֹא זָכִיתִי שֶׁתֵּאָמֵר יְצִיאַת מִצְרַיִם בַּלֵּילוֹת עַד שֶׁדְּרָשָׁהּ בֶּן זוֹמָא, שֶׁנֶּאֱמַר, לְמַעַן תִּזְכֹּר אֶת יוֹם צֵאתְךָ מֵאֶרֶץ מִצְרַיִם כֹּל יְמֵי חַיֶּיךָ. יְמֵי חַיֶּיךָ הַיָּמִים. כֹּל יְמֵי חַיֶּיךָ הַלֵּילוֹת. וַחֲכָמִים אוֹמְרִים יְמֵי חַיֶּיךָ הָעוֹלָם הַזֶּה. כֹּל יְמֵי חַיֶּיךָ לְהָבִיא לִימוֹת הַמָּשִׁיחַ:

MORNING'S HERE! THE MORNING'S HERE! SUNSHINE IS HERE, THE SKY IS CLEAR! THE MORNING'S HERE! GET INTO GEAR, BREAKFAST IS NEAR. THE DARK OF NIGHT HAS DISAPPEARED![31]

The Four Sons

Blessed be the Place [of all], Blessed be He; Blessed be the One who Gave the Torah to His people Israel, Blessed be He. Corresponding to four sons did the Torah speak; one [who is] wise, one [who is] evil, one who is innocent and one who doesn't know to ask.

What does the wise [son] say? "What are these testimonies, statutes and judgments that the Lord our God commanded you?' " And accordingly you will say to him, as per the laws of the Pesach sacrifice, "We may not eat an afikoman [a dessert or other foods eaten after the meal] after [we are finished eating] the Pesach sacrifice.

S9E21: The one with the Fertility Test
Charlie: You know, actually I'm a little surprised too, myself. I mean, Joey is so different from the guys I usually date. I mean, they're all professors, and intellectuals, and paleontologists mostly, you know, very cerebral…
Ross: Yeah, I know the type.

כנגד ארבעה בנים

בָּרוּךְ הַמָּקוֹם, בָּרוּךְ הוּא, בָּרוּךְ שֶׁנָּתַן תּוֹרָה לְעַמּוֹ יִשְׂרָאֵל, בָּרוּךְ הוּא. כְּנֶגֶד אַרְבָּעָה בָנִים דִּבְּרָה תוֹרָה: אֶחָד חָכָם, וְאֶחָד רָשָׁע, וְאֶחָד תָּם, וְאֶחָד שֶׁאֵינוֹ יוֹדֵעַ לִשְׁאוֹל.

חָכָם מָה הוּא אוֹמֵר? מָה הָעֵדוֹת וְהַחֻקִּים וְהַמִּשְׁפָּטִים אֲשֶׁר צִוָּה ה' אֱלֹהֵינוּ אֶתְכֶם. וְאַף אַתָּה אֱמוֹר לוֹ כְּהִלְכוֹת הַפֶּסַח: אֵין מַפְטִירִין אַחַר הַפֶּסַח אֲפִיקוֹמָן:

32

What does the evil [son] say? '"What is this worship to you?"' 'To you' and not 'to him.' And since he excluded himself from the collective, he denied a principle [of the Jewish faith]. And accordingly, you will blunt his teeth and say to him, '"For the sake of this, did the Lord do [this] for me in my going out of Egypt'." 'For me' and not 'for him.' If he had been there, he would not have been saved.

What does the innocent [son] say? '"What is this?' "And you will say to him, '"With the strength of [His] hand did the Lord take us out from Egypt, from the house of slaves'

רָשָׁע מָה הוּא אוֹמֵר? מָה הָעֲבוֹדָה הַזֹּאת לָכֶם. לָכֶם – וְלֹא לוֹ. וּלְפִי שֶׁהוֹצִיא אֶת עַצְמוֹ מִן הַכְּלָל כָּפַר בְּעִקָּר. וְאַף אַתָּה הַקְהֵה אֶת שִׁנָּיו וֶאֱמֹר לוֹ: "בַּעֲבוּר זֶה עָשָׂה ה' לִי בְּצֵאתִי מִמִּצְרָיִם". לִי וְלֹא-לוֹ. אִלּוּ הָיָה שָׁם, לֹא הָיָה נִגְאָל:

תָּם מָה הוּא אוֹמֵר? מַה זֹּאת? וְאָמַרְתָּ אֵלָיו "בְּחֹזֶק יָד הוֹצִיאָנוּ ה' מִמִּצְרַיִם מִבֵּית עֲבָדִים".

I'm Joey. I'm disgusting. [33]

S9E21: The one with the Fertility Test
Joey: It's just that she's so much smarter than all the girls I've ever dated! Combined! I don't want her to think I'm stupid!
Ross: (looking down) Are you wearing two belts?
Joey: (checking) EH, what do you know!
Ross: You were saying you didn't want to seem stupid.

And the one who doesn't know to ask, you will open [the conversation] for him. As it is stated, "And you will speak to your son on that day saying, for the sake of this, did the Lord do [this] for me in my going out of Egypt."

וְשֶׁאֵינוֹ יוֹדֵעַ לִשְׁאוֹל – אַתְּ פְּתַח לוֹ, שֶׁנֶּאֱמַר, וְהִגַּדְתָּ לְבִנְךָ בַּיּוֹם הַהוּא לֵאמֹר, בַּעֲבוּר זֶה עָשָׂה ה' לִי בְּצֵאתִי מִמִּצְרָיִם.

It's like a cow's opinion. It just doesn't matter. It's moo.[34]

It could be from Rosh Chodesh [that one would have to discuss the Exodus. However] we learn it is stated, "on that day." If it is [written] "on that day," it could be from while it is still day [before the night of the fifteenth of Nissan. However] we learn [otherwise, since] it is stated, "for the sake of this." I didn't say 'for the sake of this' except [that it be observed] when [this] matzah and maror are resting in front of you.

יָכוֹל מֵרֹאשׁ חֹדֶשׁ? תַּלְמוּד לוֹמַר בַּיּוֹם הַהוּא. אִי בַּיּוֹם הַהוּא יָכוֹל מִבְּעוֹד יוֹם? תַּלְמוּד לוֹמַר בַּעֲבוּר זֶה – בַּעֲבוּר זֶה לֹא אָמַרְתִּי, אֶלָּא בְּשָׁעָה שֶׁיֵּשׁ מַצָּה וּמָרוֹר מֻנָּחִים לְפָנֶיךָ.

From the beginning, our ancestors were idol worshipers. And now, the Place [of all] has brought us close to His worship, as it is stated, "Yehoshua said to the whole people, so said the Lord, God of Israel, 'Over the river did your ancestors dwell from always, Terach the father of Avraham and the father of Nachor, and they worshiped other gods.

מִתְּחִלָּה עוֹבְדֵי עֲבוֹדָה זָרָה הָיוּ אֲבוֹתֵינוּ, וְעַכְשָׁיו קֵרְבָנוּ הַמָּקוֹם לַעֲבֹדָתוֹ, שֶׁנֶּאֱמַר: וַיֹּאמֶר יְהוֹשֻׁעַ אֶל־כָּל־הָעָם, כֹּה אָמַר ה' אֱלֹהֵי יִשְׂרָאֵל: בְּעֵבֶר הַנָּהָר יָשְׁבוּ אֲבוֹתֵיכֶם מֵעוֹלָם, תֶּרַח אֲבִי אַבְרָהָם וַאֲבִי נָחוֹר, וַיַּעַבְדוּ אֱלֹהִים אֲחֵרִים.

And I took your father, Avraham, from over the river and I made him walk in all the land of Canaan and I increased his seed and I gave him Yitschak. And I gave to Yitschak, Ya'akov and Esav; and I gave to Esav, Mount Seir [in order that he] inherit it; and Yaakov and his sons went down to Egypt.'"

וָאֶקַּח אֶת־אֲבִיכֶם אֶת־אַבְרָהָם מֵעֵבֶר הַנָּהָר וָאוֹלֵךְ אוֹתוֹ בְּכָל־אֶרֶץ כְּנָעַן, וָאַרְבֶּה אֶת־זַרְעוֹ וָאֶתֵּן לוֹ אֶת־יִצְחָק, וָאֶתֵּן לְיִצְחָק אֶת־יַעֲקֹב וְאֶת־עֵשָׂו. וָאֶתֵּן לְעֵשָׂו אֶת־הַר שֵׂעִיר לָרֶשֶׁת אֹתוֹ, וְיַעֲקֹב וּבָנָיו יָרְדוּ מִצְרָיִם.

Blessed be the One who keeps His promise to Israel, blessed be He; since the Holy One, blessed be He, calculated the end [of the exile,] to do as He said to Avraham, our father, in the Covenant between the Pieces, as it is stated, "And He said to Avram, 'you should surely know that your seed will be a stranger in a land that is not theirs, and they will enslave them and afflict them four hundred years. And also that nation for which they shall toil will I judge, and afterwards they will go out with much property.'"

בָּרוּךְ שׁוֹמֵר הַבְטָחָתוֹ לְיִשְׂרָאֵל, בָּרוּךְ הוּא. שֶׁהַקָּדוֹשׁ בָּרוּךְ הוּא חִשַּׁב אֶת־הַקֵּץ, לַעֲשׂוֹת כְּמוֹ שֶׁאָמַר לְאַבְרָהָם אָבִינוּ בִּבְרִית בֵּין הַבְּתָרִים, שֶׁנֶּאֱמַר: וַיֹּאמֶר לְאַבְרָם, יָדֹעַ תֵּדַע כִּי־גֵר יִהְיֶה זַרְעֲךָ בְּאֶרֶץ לֹא לָהֶם, וַעֲבָדוּם וְעִנּוּ אֹתָם אַרְבַּע מֵאוֹת שָׁנָה. וְגַם אֶת־הַגּוֹי אֲשֶׁר יַעֲבֹדוּ דָּן אָנֹכִי וְאַחֲרֵי־כֵן יֵצְאוּ בִּרְכֻשׁ גָּדוֹל.

He covers the matzah and lifts up the cup and says:

And it is this that has stood for our ancestors and for us; since it is not [only] one [person or nation] that has stood [against] us to destroy us, but rather in each generation, they stand [against] us to destroy us, but the Holy One, blessed be He, rescues us from their hand.

He puts down the cup from his hand and uncovers the matzah.

Go out and learn what Lavan the Aramean sought to do to Ya'akov, our father; since Pharaoh only decreed [the death sentence] on the males but Lavan sought to uproot the whole [people]. As it is stated, "An Aramean was destroying my father and he went down to Egypt, and he resided there with a small number and he became there a nation, great, powerful and numerous."

"And he went down to Egypt" - helpless on account of the word [in which God told Avraham that his descendants would have to go into exile]. "And he resided there" - [this] teaches that Ya'akov, our father, didn't go down to settle in Egypt, but rather [only] to reside there, as it is stated, "And they said to Pharaoh, 'To reside in the land have we come, since there is not enough pasture for your servant's flocks, since the famine is heavy in the land of Canaan, and now please grant that your servants should dwell in the Land of Goshen.'"

מכסה המצה ומגביה את הכוס בידו, ואומר:

וְהִיא שֶׁעָמְדָה לַאֲבוֹתֵינוּ וְלָנוּ. שֶׁלֹּא אֶחָד בִּלְבָד עָמַד עָלֵינוּ לְכַלּוֹתֵנוּ, אֶלָּא שֶׁבְּכָל דּוֹר וָדוֹר עוֹמְדִים עָלֵינוּ לְכַלּוֹתֵנוּ, וְהַקָּדוֹשׁ בָּרוּךְ הוּא מַצִּילֵנוּ מִיָּדָם.

יניח הכוס מידו ויגלה את המצות.

צֵא וּלְמַד מַה בִּקֵּשׁ לָבָן הָאֲרַמִּי לַעֲשׂוֹת לְיַעֲקֹב אָבִינוּ: שֶׁפַּרְעֹה לֹא גָזַר אֶלָּא עַל הַזְּכָרִים, וְלָבָן בִּקֵּשׁ לַעֲקֹר אֶת־הַכֹּל. שֶׁנֶּאֱמַר: אֲרַמִּי אֹבֵד אָבִי, וַיֵּרֶד מִצְרַיְמָה וַיָּגָר שָׁם בִּמְתֵי מְעָט, וַיְהִי שָׁם לְגוֹי גָּדוֹל, עָצוּם וָרָב.

וַיֵּרֶד מִצְרַיְמָה – אָנוּס עַל פִּי הַדִּבּוּר. וַיָּגָר שָׁם. מְלַמֵּד שֶׁלֹּא יָרַד יַעֲקֹב אָבִינוּ לְהִשְׁתַּקֵּעַ בְּמִצְרַיִם אֶלָּא לָגוּר שָׁם, שֶׁנֶּאֱמַר: וַיֹּאמְרוּ אֶל־פַּרְעֹה, לָגוּר בָּאָרֶץ בָּאנוּ, כִּי אֵין מִרְעֶה לַצֹּאן אֲשֶׁר לַעֲבָדֶיךָ, כִּי כָבֵד הָרָעָב בְּאֶרֶץ כְּנָעַן. וְעַתָּה יֵשְׁבוּ־נָא עֲבָדֶיךָ בְּאֶרֶץ גֹּשֶׁן.

בִּמְתֵי מְעָט. כְּמָה שֶׁנֶּאֱמַר: בְּשִׁבְעִים נֶפֶשׁ יָרְדוּ אֲבוֹתֶיךָ מִצְרָיְמָה, וְעַתָּה שָׂמְךָ ה' אֱלֹהֶיךָ כְּכוֹכְבֵי הַשָּׁמַיִם לָרֹב.

וַיְהִי שָׁם לְגוֹי. מְלַמֵּד שֶׁהָיוּ יִשְׂרָאֵל מְצֻיָּנִים שָׁם. גָּדוֹל עָצוּם – כְּמָה שֶׁנֶּאֱמַר: וּבְנֵי יִשְׂרָאֵל פָּרוּ וַיִּשְׁרְצוּ וַיִּרְבּוּ וַיַּעַצְמוּ בִּמְאֹד מְאֹד, וַתִּמָּלֵא הָאָרֶץ אֹתָם.

וָרָב. כְּמָה שֶׁנֶּאֱמַר: רְבָבָה כְּצֶמַח הַשָּׂדֶה נְתַתִּיךְ, וַתִּרְבִּי וַתִּגְדְּלִי וַתָּבֹאִי בַּעֲדִי עֲדָיִים, שָׁדַיִם נָכֹנוּ וּשְׂעָרֵךְ צִמֵּחַ, וְאַתְּ עֵרֹם וְעֶרְיָה. וָאֶעֱבֹר עָלַיִךְ וָאֶרְאֵךְ מִתְבּוֹסֶסֶת בְּדָמָיִךְ, וָאֹמַר לָךְ בְּדָמַיִךְ חֲיִי, וָאֹמַר לָךְ בְּדָמַיִךְ חֲיִי.

וַיָּרֵעוּ אֹתָנוּ הַמִּצְרִים וַיְעַנּוּנוּ, וַיִּתְּנוּ עָלֵינוּ עֲבֹדָה קָשָׁה. וַיָּרֵעוּ אֹתָנוּ הַמִּצְרִים – כְּמָה שֶׁנֶּאֱמַר: הָבָה נִתְחַכְּמָה לוֹ פֶּן יִרְבֶּה, וְהָיָה כִּי תִקְרֶאנָה מִלְחָמָה וְנוֹסַף גַּם הוּא עַל שֹׂנְאֵינוּ וְנִלְחַם־בָּנוּ, וְעָלָה מִן־הָאָרֶץ.

וַיְעַנּוּנוּ. כְּמָה שֶׁנֶּאֱמַר: וַיָּשִׂימוּ עָלָיו שָׂרֵי מִסִּים לְמַעַן עַנֹּתוֹ בְּסִבְלֹתָם. וַיִּבֶן עָרֵי מִסְכְּנוֹת לְפַרְעֹה, אֶת־פִּתֹם וְאֶת־רַעַמְסֵס.

וַיִּתְּנוּ עָלֵינוּ עֲבֹדָה קָשָׁה. כְּמָה שֶׁנֶּאֱמַר: וַיַּעֲבִדוּ מִצְרַיִם אֶת־בְּנֵי יִשְׂרָאֵל בְּפָרֶךְ.

וַנִּצְעַק אֶל־ה' אֱלֹהֵי אֲבֹתֵינוּ, וַיִּשְׁמַע ה' אֶת־קֹלֵנוּ, וַיַּרְא אֶת־עָנְיֵנוּ וְאֶת עֲמָלֵנוּ וְאֶת לַחֲצֵנוּ.

"As a small number" - as it is stated, "With seventy souls did your ancestors come down to Egypt, and now the Lord your God has made you as numerous as the stars of the sky."

"And he became there a nation" - [this] teaches that Israel [became] distinguishable there. "Great, powerful" - as it is stated, "And the Children of Israel multiplied and swarmed and grew numerous and strong, most exceedingly and the land became full of them."

"And numerous" - as it is stated, "I have given you to be numerous as the vegetation of the field, and you increased and grew and became highly ornamented, your breasts were set and your hair grew, but you were naked and barren." "And when I passed by thee, and saw thee weltering in thy blood, I said to thee, In thy blood live! yea, I said to thee, In thy blood live!"

"And the Egyptians did bad to us" - as it is stated, "Let us be wise towards him, lest he multiply and it will be that when war is called, he too will join with our enemies and fight against us and go up from the land."

"And afflicted us" - as is is stated; "And they placed upon him leaders over the work-tax in order to afflict them with their burdens; and they built storage cities, Pithom and Ra'amses."

"And put upon us hard work" - as it is stated, "And they enslaved the children of Israel with breaking work."

"And we we cried out to the Lord, the God of our ancestors, and the Lord heard our voice, and He saw our affliction, and our toil and our duress".

וַנִּצְעַק אֶל ה' אֱלֹהֵי אֲבֹתֵינוּ – כְּמָה שֶׁנֶּאֱמַר: וַיְהִי בַיָּמִים הָרַבִּים הָהֵם וַיָּמָת מֶלֶךְ מִצְרַיִם, וַיֵּאָנְחוּ בְנֵי־יִשְׂרָאֵל מִן־הָעֲבוֹדָה וַיִּזְעָקוּ, וַתַּעַל שַׁוְעָתָם אֶל־הָאֱלֹהִים מִן הָעֲבֹדָה.

"And we cried out to the Lord, the God of our ancestors" - as it is stated; "And it was in those great days that the king of Egypt died and the Children of Israel sighed from the work and yelled out, and their supplication went up to God from the work."

וַיִּשְׁמַע ה' אֶת קֹלֵנוּ. כְּמָה שֶׁנֶּאֱמַר: וַיִּשְׁמַע אֱלֹהִים אֶת־נַאֲקָתָם, וַיִּזְכֹּר אֱלֹהִים אֶת־בְּרִיתוֹ אֶת־אַבְרָהָם, אֶת־יִצְחָק וְאֶת־יַעֲקֹב.

"And the Lord heard our voice" - as it is stated; "And God heard their groans and God remembered His covenant with Avraham and with Yitschak and with Ya'akov."

וַיַּרְא אֶת־עָנְיֵנוּ. זוֹ פְּרִישׁוּת דֶּרֶךְ אֶרֶץ, כְּמָה שֶׁנֶּאֱמַר: וַיַּרְא אֱלֹהִים אֶת בְּנֵי־יִשְׂרָאֵל וַיֵּדַע אֱלֹהִים.

"And He saw our affliction" - this [refers to] the separation from the way of the world, as it is stated; "And God saw the Children of Israel and God knew."

וְאֶת־עֲמָלֵנוּ. אֵלוּ הַבָּנִים. כְּמָה שֶׁנֶּאֱמַר: כָּל־הַבֵּן הַיִּלּוֹד הַיְאֹרָה תַּשְׁלִיכֻהוּ וְכָל־הַבַּת תְּחַיּוּן.

"And our toil" - this [refers to the killing of the] sons, as it is stated; "Every boy that is born, throw him into the Nile and every girl you shall keep alive."

וְאֶת לַחֲצֵנוּ. זֶו הַדְּחַק, כְּמָה שֶׁנֶּאֱמַר: וְגַם־רָאִיתִי אֶת־הַלַּחַץ אֲשֶׁר מִצְרַיִם לֹחֲצִים אֹתָם.

"And our duress" - this [refers to] the pressure, as it is stated; "And I also saw the duress that the Egyptians are applying on them."

וַיּוֹצִאֵנוּ ה' מִמִּצְרַיִם בְּיָד חֲזָקָה, וּבִזְרֹעַ נְטוּיָה, וּבְמֹרָא גָּדֹל, וּבְאֹתוֹת וּבְמֹפְתִים.

"And the Lord took us out of Egypt with a strong hand and with an outstretched forearm and with great awe and with signs and with wonders".

וַיּוֹצִאֵנוּ ה' מִמִּצְרַיִם. לֹא עַל־יְדֵי מַלְאָךְ, וְלֹא עַל־יְדֵי שָׂרָף, וְלֹא עַל־יְדֵי שָׁלִיחַ, אֶלָּא הַקָּדוֹשׁ בָּרוּךְ הוּא בִּכְבוֹדוֹ וּבְעַצְמוֹ. שֶׁנֶּאֱמַר: וְעָבַרְתִּי בְאֶרֶץ מִצְרַיִם בַּלַּיְלָה הַזֶּה, וְהִכֵּיתִי כָל־בְּכוֹר בְּאֶרֶץ מִצְרַיִם מֵאָדָם וְעַד בְּהֵמָה, וּבְכָל אֱלֹהֵי מִצְרַיִם אֶעֱשֶׂה שְׁפָטִים. אֲנִי ה'.

"And the Lord took us out of Egypt" - not through an angel and not through a seraph and not through a messenger, but [directly by] the Holy One, blessed be He, Himself, as it is stated; "And I will pass through the Land of Egypt on that night and I will smite every firstborn in the Land of Egypt, from men to animals; and with all the gods of Egypt, I will make judgments, I am the Lord."

"And I will pass through the Land of Egypt" - I and not an angel. "And I will smite every firstborn" - I and not a seraph. "And with all the gods of Egypt, I will make judgments" - I and not a messenger. "I am the Lord" - I am He and there is no other.

וְעָבַרְתִּי בְאֶרֶץ מִצְרַיִם בַּלַּיְלָה הַזֶּה – אֲנִי וְלֹא מַלְאָךְ; וְהִכֵּיתִי כָל בְּכוֹר בְּאֶרֶץ־מִצְרַיִם. אֲנִי וְלֹא שָׂרָף; וּבְכָל־אֱלֹהֵי מִצְרַיִם אֶעֱשֶׂה שְׁפָטִים. אֲנִי וְלֹא הַשָּׁלִיחַ; אֲנִי ה'. אֲנִי הוּא וְלֹא אַחֵר.

"With a strong hand" - this [refers to] the pestilence, as it is stated; "Behold the hand of the Lord is upon your herds that are in the field, upon the horses, upon the donkeys, upon the camels, upon the cattle and upon the flocks, [there will be] a very heavy pestilence."

בְּיָד חֲזָקָה. זוֹ הַדֶּבֶר, כְּמָה שֶׁנֶּאֱמַר: הִנֵּה יַד־ה' הוֹיָה בְּמִקְנְךָ אֲשֶׁר בַּשָּׂדֶה, בַּסּוּסִים, בַּחֲמֹרִים, בַּגְּמַלִּים, בַּבָּקָר וּבַצֹּאן, דֶּבֶר כָּבֵד מְאֹד.

"And with an outstretched forearm" - this [refers to] the sword, as it is stated; "And his sword was drawn in his hand, leaning over Jerusalem."

וּבִזְרֹעַ נְטוּיָה. זוֹ הַחֶרֶב, כְּמָה שֶׁנֶּאֱמַר: וְחַרְבּוֹ שְׁלוּפָה בְּיָדוֹ, נְטוּיָה עַל־יְרוּשָׁלָיִם.

"And with great awe" - this [refers to the revelation of] the Divine Presence, as it is stated, "Or did God try to take for Himself a nation from within a nation with enigmas, with signs and with wonders and with war and with a strong hand and with an outstretched forearm and with great and awesome acts, like all that the Lord, your God, did for you in Egypt in front of your eyes?"

וּבְמוֹרָא גָּדֹל. זוֹ גִּלּוּי שְׁכִינָה. כְּמָה שֶׁנֶּאֱמַר, אוֹ הֲנִסָּה אֱלֹהִים לָבוֹא לָקַחַת לוֹ גוֹי מִקֶּרֶב גּוֹי בְּמַסֹּת בְּאֹתֹת וּבְמוֹפְתִים וּבְמִלְחָמָה וּבְיָד חֲזָקָה וּבִזְרוֹעַ נְטוּיָה וּבְמוֹרָאִים גְּדֹלִים כְּכֹל אֲשֶׁר־עָשָׂה לָכֶם ה' אֱלֹהֵיכֶם בְּמִצְרַיִם לְעֵינֶיךָ.

"And with signs" - this [refers to] the staff, as it is stated; "And this staff you shall take in your hand, that with it you will perform signs."

וּבְאֹתוֹת. זֶה הַמַּטֶּה, כְּמָה שֶׁנֶּאֱמַר: וְאֶת הַמַּטֶּה הַזֶּה תִּקַּח בְּיָדְךָ, אֲשֶׁר תַּעֲשֶׂה־בּוֹ אֶת הָאֹתֹת.

"And with wonders" - this [refers to] the blood, as it is stated; "And I will place my wonders in the skies and in the earth:

וּבְמֹפְתִים. זֶה הַדָּם, כְּמָה שֶׁנֶּאֱמַר: וְנָתַתִּי מוֹפְתִים בַּשָּׁמַיִם וּבָאָרֶץ.

Leaving Egypt

S4E15: The One With All The Rugby
Janice: I'll write you everyday.
15 Yemen Road, Yemen.

S4E23: The One with Ross's Wedding Part 1
Monica: Guys, hurry up! The flight leaves in 4 hours, it can take time to get a taxi, there could be traffic, the plane could leave early! When we get to "the holy land" (London) there could be a line at customs! Come on!
Chandler: 6 hour flight to The Holy Land (London), that's a lot of Monica.
Monica: Passport, check! Camera, check! Traveler's checks, check!
Ross: Hey! Are you ready yet?
Monica: Yup, you got the tickets?
Ross: I got em right here, check!
Joey: It's all the Holy Land (London), baby! Here we go! *snaps picture of Chandler*
Chandler: You got your passport?
Joey: Yeah! In my third drawer on my dresser, you don't want to lose that!
Chandler gives Joey a look… wait for it
Joey: Oh!
Chandler: There it is!

Outstretched Arm

S3E8: The One With the Giant Poking Device
Phoebe: Woo-Hoo! The curse is broken! I called everybody I know, and everyone is alive.
Joey: Uh...
Phoebe: What?
Joey: Ugly Naked Guy looks awfully still.
(Phoebe runs to the window and gasps.)
Phoebe: Oh my God! I killed him! I killed another one! And this curse is getting stronger too, to bring down something that big.
Rachel: Well maybe he's just taking a nap.
Joey: I'm tellin' ya, he hasn't moved since this morning.
Monica: All right, we should call somebody.
Ross: And tell them what? The naked guy we stare at all the time isn't moving.
Rachel: Well, we have gotta find out if he's alive.
Monica: How are we gonna do that? There's no way.
Joey: Well, there is one way. His window's open, I say, we poke him.

Signs

S4E23: The One After Vegas
Monica: Wow! I can't believe I actually rolled an eight.
Chandler: That was so unlikely. Well, let's get married! I guess.
Monica: Wait a minute. That wasn't a hard eight! Last night I rolled a hard eight.
Chandler: That's right! It was the wrong kind of eight, no wedding! Damnit!
Monica: I wanted it so bad! (Pause) Wanna go pack?
Chandler: Yeah. (They go pack.) We're doing the right thing, right?
Monica: Ohh, of course we are! (They walk up to the elevators.) We left it up to fate. (Pushes the elevator button.) If we were supposed to get married there would be a **clear-cut sign!** (The elevator door opens to a priest reading from a bible with Chandler and Monica standing side-by-side holding each other's hands.)

10 MAKOT, MAKOT 10
THE MITZRIM WERE PUNISHED AGAIN AND AGAIN

The Ten Plagues

And when he says, "blood and fire and pillars of smoke" and the ten plagues and "detsakh," "adash" and "ba'achab," he should pour out a little wine from his cup.

"Blood and fire and pillars of smoke."

Another [explanation]: "With a strong hand" [corresponds to] two [plagues]; "and with an outstretched forearm" [corresponds to] two [plagues]; "and with great awe" [corresponds to] two [plagues]; "and with signs" [corresponds to] two [plagues]; "and with wonders" [corresponds to] two [plagues].

These are [the] ten plagues that the Holy One, blessed be He, brought on the Egyptians in Egypt and they are:

עשרת המכות

כשאומר דם ואש ותימרות עשן, עשר המכות ודצ"ך עד"ש באח"ב – ישפוך מן הכוס מעט יין:

דָּם וָאֵשׁ וְתִימְרוֹת עָשָׁן.

דָּבָר אַחֵר: בְּיָד חֲזָקָה שְׁתַּיִם, וּבִזְרֹעַ נְטוּיָה שְׁתַּיִם, וּבְמֹרָא גָּדֹל – שְׁתַּיִם, וּבְאֹתוֹת – שְׁתַּיִם, וּבְמֹפְתִים – שְׁתַּיִם.

אֵלּוּ עֶשֶׂר מַכּוֹת שֶׁהֵבִיא הַקָּדוֹשׁ בָּרוּךְ הוּא עַל־הַמִּצְרִים בְּמִצְרַיִם, וְאֵלּוּ הֵן:

Blood דָּם

I'm a blood relative.
BLOOD!³⁶

Frogs צְפַרְדֵּעַ

³⁷

Lice כִּנִּים

³⁸

עָרוֹב

Wild Animals

Pestilence דֶּבֶר

43

S9E20: The One with the Soap Opera Party
Rachel: Oh, hi! I would shake your hand but... I'm sure you don't want to get my chicken disease!

Boils שְׁחִין

44

S6E7: The One Where Phoebe Runs
(Monica comes home and Chandler is trying to put all of the furniture back in exactly the right way.)
Chandler: (closing the door on Monica) No no no, you can't come in here! Ah Ross is naked!
Monica: What?
Ross: What?
Chandler: I couldn't say that I was naked because she's allowed to see me naked.
Ross: Why does anyone have to be naked?
Monica: Why is Ross naked?
Ross: I...I had to...show Chandler something
Monica: Naked?
Ross: I guess I have a guy problem
Monica: Is it the same thing that Chandler had?
(Ross and Chandler stare awkwardly at each other)
Chandler: Look, just come back later, we'll get everything squared away and you can come back later!
Monica: Ok, hey listen, there's still some of Chandler's medicine left under the sink in the bathroom. Bye!
Chandler: Bye!... Thank god.

Ross: Dude, what'd you have?

Hail בָּרָד

Phoebe, what do you think a good stage name for me would be?

Flameboy!

אַרְבֶּה
Locusts

Darkness חֹשֶׁךְ

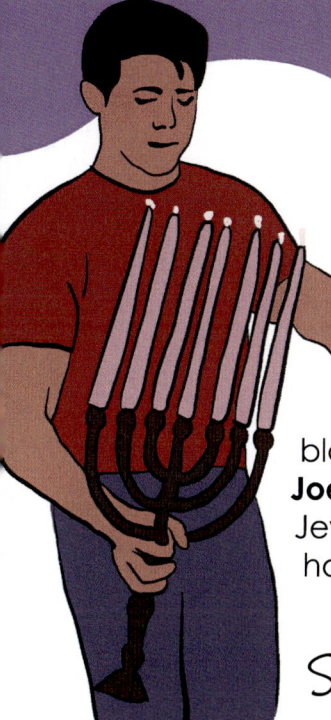

S1E7: The One with the Blackout
(Joey finds a long-lost Menorah to shine light in Monica's apartment during the blackout.)

Ross: And officiating at tonight's blackout, Rabbi Tribbiani!
Joey: Well, Chandlers last roommate was Jewish and these are the only candles we have, so happy Hanukkah everyone.

Slaying of the Firstborn מַכַּת בְּכוֹרוֹת

S6E4: The One Where Joey Loses His Insurance
Chandler: Hey, what's the matter?
Phoebe: Well, you know that psychic I see? Well, she told me that I'm going to die this week so I'm kind of bummed about that.
Chandler: What?
Phoebe: Yeah, and I know you guys don't know a lot about psychic readings, but that one is pretty much the worse one you can get.
(Later that day)
Phoebe: Hey, listen to this! My reading was wrong. I'm not going to die.
Rachel: Really? How do you know?
Phoebe: Because my psychic is dead. She must have read the cards wrong!
Rachel: Oh I'm sorry!
Phoebe: Eh, better her than me, let's bake cookies!

It's so exhausting, waiting for death.

Rabbi Yehuda was accustomed to giving [the plagues] mnemonics: Detsakh, Adash, Beachav.

Rabbi Yose Hagelili says, "From where can you [derive] that the Egyptians were struck with ten plagues in Egypt and struck with fifty plagues at the Sea? In Egypt, what does it state? 'Then the magicians said unto Pharaoh: 'This is the finger of God'. And at the Sea, what does it state? 'And Israel saw the Lord's great hand that he used upon the Egyptians, and the people feared the Lord; and they believed in the Lord, and in Moshe, His servant'. How many were they struck with with the finger? Ten plagues. You can say from here that in Egypt, they were struck with ten plagues and at the Sea, they were struck with fifty plagues."

רַבִּי יְהוּדָה הָיָה נוֹתֵן בָּהֶם סִמָּנִים: דְּצַ״ךְ עַדַ״שׁ בְּאַחַ״ב.

רַבִּי יוֹסֵי הַגְּלִילִי אוֹמֵר: מִנַּיִן אַתָּה אוֹמֵר שֶׁלָּקוּ הַמִּצְרִים בְּמִצְרַיִם עֶשֶׂר מַכּוֹת וְעַל הַיָּם לָקוּ חֲמִשִּׁים מַכּוֹת? בְּמִצְרַיִם מָה הוּא אוֹמֵר? וַיֹּאמְרוּ הַחַרְטֻמִּם אֶל פַּרְעֹה: אֶצְבַּע אֱלֹהִים הִוא, וְעַל הַיָּם מָה הוּא אוֹמֵר? וַיַּרְא יִשְׂרָאֵל אֶת־הַיָּד הַגְּדֹלָה אֲשֶׁר עָשָׂה ה' בְּמִצְרַיִם, וַיִּירְאוּ הָעָם אֶת־ה', וַיַּאֲמִינוּ בַּיי וּבְמֹשֶׁה עַבְדּוֹ. כַּמָּה לָקוּ בְאֶצְבַּע? עֶשֶׂר מַכּוֹת. אֱמֹר מֵעַתָּה: בְּמִצְרַיִם לָקוּ עֶשֶׂר מַכּוֹת וְעַל הַיָּם לָקוּ חֲמִשִּׁים מַכּוֹת.

Rabbi Eliezer says, "From where [can you derive] that every plague that the Holy One, blessed be He, brought upon the Egyptians in Egypt was [composed] of four plagues? As it is stated: 'He sent upon them the fierceness of His anger, wrath, and fury, and trouble, a sending of messengers of evil.' 'Wrath' [corresponds to] one; 'and fury' [brings it to] two; 'and trouble' [brings it to] three; 'a sending of messengers of evil' [brings it to] four. You can say from here that in Egypt, they were struck with forty plagues and at the Sea, they were struck with two hundred plagues."

רַבִּי אֱלִיעֶזֶר אוֹמֵר: מִנַּיִן שֶׁכָּל־מַכָּה וּמַכָּה שֶׁהֵבִיא הַקָּדוֹשׁ בָּרוּךְ הוּא עַל הַמִּצְרִים בְּמִצְרַיִם הָיְתָה שֶׁל אַרְבַּע מַכּוֹת? שֶׁנֶּאֱמַר: יְשַׁלַּח־בָּם חֲרוֹן אַפּוֹ, עֶבְרָה וָזַעַם וְצָרָה, מִשְׁלַחַת מַלְאֲכֵי רָעִים. עֶבְרָה – אַחַת, וָזַעַם – שְׁתַּיִם, וְצָרָה – שָׁלֹשׁ, מִשְׁלַחַת מַלְאֲכֵי רָעִים – אַרְבַּע. אֱמוֹר מֵעַתָּה: בְּמִצְרַיִם לָקוּ אַרְבָּעִים מַכּוֹת וְעַל הַיָּם לָקוּ מָאתַיִם מַכּוֹת.

Rabbi Akiva says, says, "From where [can you derive] that every plague that the Holy One, blessed be He, brought upon the Egyptians in Egypt was [composed] of five plagues? As it is stated: 'He sent upon them the fierceness of His anger, wrath, and fury, and trouble, a sending of messengers of evil.' 'The fierceness of His anger' [corresponds to] one; 'wrath' [brings it to] two; 'and fury' [brings it to] three; 'and trouble' [brings it to] four; 'a sending of messengers of evil' [brings it to] five. You can say from here that in Egypt, they were struck with fifty plagues and at the Sea, they were struck with two hundred and fifty plagues."

רַבִּי עֲקִיבָא אוֹמֵר: מִנַּיִן שֶׁכָּל־מַכָּה וּמַכָּה שֶׁהֵבִיא הַקָּדוֹשׁ בָּרוּךְ הוּא עַל הַמִּצְרִים בְּמִצְרַיִם הָיְתָה שֶׁל חָמֵשׁ מַכּוֹת? שֶׁנֶּאֱמַר: יְשַׁלַּח־בָּם חֲרוֹן אַפּוֹ, עֶבְרָה וָזַעַם וְצָרָה, מִשְׁלַחַת מַלְאֲכֵי רָעִים. חֲרוֹן אַפּוֹ – אַחַת, עֶבְרָה – שְׁתַּיִם, וָזַעַם – שָׁלוֹשׁ, וְצָרָה – אַרְבַּע, מִשְׁלַחַת מַלְאֲכֵי רָעִים – חָמֵשׁ. אֱמוֹר מֵעַתָּה: בְּמִצְרַיִם לָקוּ חֲמִשִּׁים מַכּוֹת וְעַל הַיָּם לָקוּ חֲמִשִּׁים וּמָאתַיִם מַכּוֹת.

Dayenu

How many degrees of good did the Place [of all bestow] upon us!

If He had taken us out of Egypt and not made judgements on them; [it would have been] enough for us.

If He had made judgments on them and had not made [them] on their gods; [it would have been] enough for us.

If He had made [them] on their gods and had not killed their firstborn; [it would have been] enough for us.

If He had killed their firstborn and had not given us their money; [it would have been] enough for us.

If He had given us their money and had not split the Sea for us; [it would have been] enough for us.

If He had split the Sea for us and had not taken us through it on dry land; [it would have been] enough for us.

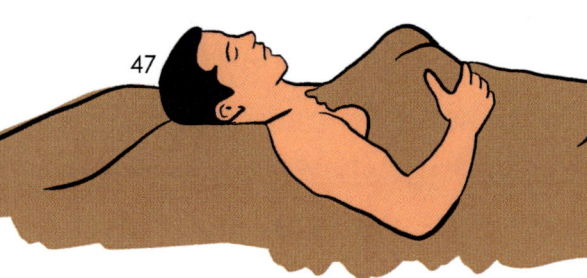

If He had taken us through it on dry land and had not pushed down our enemies in [the Sea]; [it would have been] enough for us.

If He had pushed down our enemies in [the Sea] and had not supplied our needs in the wilderness for forty years; [it would have been] enough for us.

דינו

כַּמָּה מַעֲלוֹת טוֹבוֹת לַמָּקוֹם עָלֵינוּ!

אִלּוּ הוֹצִיאָנוּ מִמִּצְרַיִם וְלֹא עָשָׂה בָהֶם שְׁפָטִים, דַּיֵּנוּ.

אִלּוּ עָשָׂה בָהֶם שְׁפָטִים, וְלֹא עָשָׂה בֵאלֹהֵיהֶם, דַּיֵּנוּ.

אִלּוּ עָשָׂה בֵאלֹהֵיהֶם, וְלֹא הָרַג אֶת־בְּכוֹרֵיהֶם, דַּיֵּנוּ.

אִלּוּ הָרַג אֶת־בְּכוֹרֵיהֶם וְלֹא נָתַן לָנוּ אֶת־מָמוֹנָם, דַּיֵּנוּ.

אִלּוּ נָתַן לָנוּ אֶת־מָמוֹנָם וְלֹא קָרַע לָנוּ אֶת־הַיָּם, דַּיֵּנוּ.

אִלּוּ קָרַע לָנוּ אֶת־הַיָּם וְלֹא הֶעֱבִירָנוּ בְּתוֹכוֹ בֶּחָרָבָה, דַּיֵּנוּ.

אִלּוּ הֶעֱבִירָנוּ בְּתוֹכוֹ בֶּחָרָבָה וְלֹא שִׁקַּע צָרֵנוּ בְּתוֹכוֹ דַּיֵּנוּ.

אִלּוּ שִׁקַּע צָרֵנוּ בְּתוֹכוֹ וְלֹא סִפֵּק צָרְכֵּנוּ בַּמִּדְבָּר אַרְבָּעִים שָׁנָה דַּיֵּנוּ.

If He had supplied our needs in the wilderness for forty years and had not fed us the manna; [it would have been] enough for us.

If He had fed us the manna and had not given us the Shabbat; [it would have been] enough for us.

אִלּוּ סִפֵּק צָרְכֵּנוּ בְּמִדְבָּר אַרְבָּעִים שָׁנָה וְלֹא הֶאֱכִילָנוּ אֶת־הַמָּן דַּיֵּנוּ.

אִלּוּ הֶאֱכִילָנוּ אֶת־הַמָּן וְלֹא נָתַן לָנוּ אֶת־הַשַּׁבָּת, דַּיֵּנוּ.

S1E1: The One Where Monica Gets a New Roommate
Joey: What are you talking about? 'One woman'? That's like saying there's only one flavor of ice cream for you. Lemme tell you something, Ross. There's lots of flavors out there. There's Rocky Road, and Cookie Dough, and Bing! Cherry Vanilla. You could get 'em with Jimmies, or nuts, or whipped cream! This is the best thing that ever happened to you! You got married, you were, like, what, eight? Welcome back to the world! Grab a spoon!

If He had given us the Shabbat and had not brought us close to Mount Sinai; [it would have been] enough for us.

If He had brought us close to Mount Sinai and had not given us the Torah; [it would have been] enough for us.

If He had given us the Torah and had not brought us into the land of Israel; [it would have been] enough for us.

If He had brought us into the land of Israel and had not built us the 'Chosen House' [the Temple; it would have been] enough for us.

אִלּוּ נָתַן לָנוּ אֶת־הַשַּׁבָּת, וְלֹא קֵרְבָנוּ לִפְנֵי הַר סִינַי, דַּיֵּנוּ.

אִלּוּ קֵרְבָנוּ לִפְנֵי הַר סִינַי, וְלֹא נָתַן לָנוּ אֶת־הַתּוֹרָה. דַּיֵּנוּ.

אִלּוּ נָתַן לָנוּ אֶת־הַתּוֹרָה וְלֹא הִכְנִיסָנוּ לְאֶרֶץ יִשְׂרָאֵל, דַּיֵּנוּ.

אִלּוּ הִכְנִיסָנוּ לְאֶרֶץ יִשְׂרָאֵל וְלֹא בָנָה לָנוּ אֶת־בֵּית הַבְּחִירָה דַּיֵּנוּ.

How much more so is the good that is doubled and quadrupled that the Place [of all bestowed] upon us [enough for us]; since he took us out of Egypt, and made judgments with them, and made [them] with their gods, and killed their firstborn, and gave us their money, and split the Sea for us, and brought us through it on dry land, and pushed down our enemies in [the Sea], and supplied our needs in the wilderness for forty years, and fed us the manna, and gave us the Shabbat, and brought us close to Mount Sinai, and gave us the Torah, and brought us into the land of Israel and built us the 'Chosen House' [the Temple] to atone upon all of our sins.

עַל אַחַת, כַּמָּה וְכַמָּה, טוֹבָה כְפוּלָה וּמְכֻפֶּלֶת לַמָּקוֹם עָלֵינוּ: שֶׁהוֹצִיאָנוּ מִמִּצְרַיִם, וְעָשָׂה בָהֶם שְׁפָטִים, וְעָשָׂה בֵאלֹהֵיהֶם, וְהָרַג אֶת־בְּכוֹרֵיהֶם, וְנָתַן לָנוּ אֶת־מָמוֹנָם, וְקָרַע לָנוּ אֶת־הַיָּם, וְהֶעֱבִירָנוּ בְּתוֹכוֹ בֶּחָרָבָה, וְשִׁקַּע צָרֵנוּ בְּתוֹכוֹ, וְסִפֵּק צָרְכֵּנוּ בַּמִּדְבָּר אַרְבָּעִים שָׁנָה, וְהֶאֱכִילָנוּ אֶת־הַמָּן, וְנָתַן לָנוּ אֶת־הַשַּׁבָּת, וְקֵרְבָנוּ לִפְנֵי הַר סִינַי, וְנָתַן לָנוּ אֶת־הַתּוֹרָה, וְהִכְנִיסָנוּ לְאֶרֶץ יִשְׂרָאֵל, וּבָנָה לָנוּ אֶת־בֵּית הַבְּחִירָה לְכַפֵּר עַל־כָּל־עֲוֹנוֹתֵינוּ.

Pesach, Matzah, and Maror

פסח מצה ומרור

Rabban Gamliel was accustomed to say, Anyone who has not said these three things on Pesach has not fulfilled his obligation, and these are them: the Pesach sacrifice, matzah and marror.

רַבָּן גַּמְלִיאֵל הָיָה אוֹמֵר: כָּל שֶׁלֹּא אָמַר שְׁלֹשָׁה דְּבָרִים אֵלּוּ בַּפֶּסַח, לֹא יָצָא יְדֵי חוֹבָתוֹ, וְאֵלּוּ הֵן: פֶּסַח, מַצָּה, וּמָרוֹר.

The Passover Sacrifice פֶּסַח

S5E9: The One with Ross's Sandwich

Joey: Well, I think we've all learned something about who's disgusting and who's not. Eh? All right, now, I'm going to get back to my bucket. I'm only eating the skin, so the chicken's up for grabs.

The Pesach [passover] sacrifice that our ancestors were accustomed to eating when the Temple existed, for the sake of what [was it]? For the sake [to commemorate] that the Holy One, blessed be He, passed over the homes of our ancestors in Egypt, as it is stated; "And you shall say: 'It is the passover sacrifice to the Lord, for that He passed over the homes of the Children of Israel in Egypt, when He smote the Egyptians, and our homes he saved.' And the people bowed the head and bowed."

פֶּסַח שֶׁהָיוּ אֲבוֹתֵינוּ אוֹכְלִים בִּזְמַן שֶׁבֵּית הַמִּקְדָּשׁ הָיָה קַיָּם, עַל שׁוּם מָה? עַל שׁוּם שֶׁפָּסַח הַקָּדוֹשׁ בָּרוּךְ הוּא עַל בָּתֵּי אֲבוֹתֵינוּ בְּמִצְרַיִם, שֶׁנֶּאֱמַר: וַאֲמַרְתֶּם זֶבַח פֶּסַח הוּא לַיי, אֲשֶׁר פָּסַח עַל בָּתֵּי בְנֵי יִשְׂרָאֵל בְּמִצְרַיִם בְּנָגְפּוֹ אֶת־מִצְרַיִם, וְאֶת־בָּתֵּינוּ הִצִּיל וַיִּקֹּד הָעָם וַיִּשְׁתַּחֲווּ.

מַצָּה Matzah

אוחז המצה בידו ומראה אותה למסובין:

He holds the matzah in his hand and shows it to the others there.

מַצָּה זוֹ שֶׁאָנוּ אוֹכְלִים, עַל שׁוּם מָה? עַל שׁוּם שֶׁלֹּא הִסְפִּיק בְּצֵקָם שֶׁל אֲבוֹתֵינוּ לְהַחֲמִיץ עַד שֶׁנִּגְלָה עֲלֵיהֶם מֶלֶךְ מַלְכֵי הַמְּלָכִים, הַקָּדוֹשׁ בָּרוּךְ הוּא, וּגְאָלָם, שֶׁנֶּאֱמַר: וַיֹּאפוּ אֶת־הַבָּצֵק אֲשֶׁר הוֹצִיאוּ מִמִּצְרַיִם עֻגֹת מַצּוֹת, כִּי לֹא חָמֵץ, כִּי גֹרְשׁוּ מִמִּצְרַיִם וְלֹא יָכְלוּ לְהִתְמַהְמֵהַּ, וְגַם צֵדָה לֹא עָשׂוּ לָהֶם.

This matzah that we are eating, for the sake of what [is it]? For the sake [to commemorate] that our ancestors' dough was not yet able to rise, before the King of the kings of kings, the Holy One, blessed be He, revealed [Himself] to them and redeemed them, as it is stated; "And they baked the dough which they brought out of Egypt into matzah cakes, since it did not rise; because they were expelled from Egypt, and could not tarry, neither had they made for themselves provisions."

Check it out. Jam Crackers![48]

מָרוֹר
Bitter Herbs

He holds the marror in his hand and shows it to the others there.

This marror [bitter greens] that we are eating, for the sake of what [is it]? For the sake [to commemorate] that the Egyptians embittered the lives of our ancestors in Egypt, as it is stated; "And they made their lives bitter with hard service, in mortar and in brick, and in all manner of service in the field; in all their service, wherein they made them serve with rigor."

אוֹחֵז הַמָּרוֹר בְּיָדוֹ וּמַרְאֶה אוֹתוֹ לַמְּסֻבִּין:

מָרוֹר זֶה שֶׁאָנוּ אוֹכְלִים, עַל שׁוּם מַה? עַל שׁוּם שֶׁמֵּרְרוּ הַמִּצְרִים אֶת־חַיֵּי אֲבוֹתֵינוּ בְּמִצְרָיִם, שֶׁנֶּאֱמַר: וַיְמָרְרוּ אֶת חַיֵּיהֶם בַּעֲבֹדָה קָשָׁה, בְּחֹמֶר וּבִלְבֵנִים וּבְכָל־עֲבֹדָה בַּשָּׂדֶה אֵת כָּל עֲבֹדָתָם אֲשֶׁר עָבְדוּ בָהֶם בְּפָרֶךְ.

In each and every generation, a person is obligated to see himself as if he left Egypt, as it is stated; "And you shall explain to your son on that day: For the sake of this, did the Lord do [this] for me in my going out of Egypt." Not only our ancestors did the Holy One, blessed be He, redeem, but rather also us [together] with them did He redeem, as it is stated; "And He took us out from there, in order to bring us in, to give us the land which He swore unto our fathers."

בְּכָל־דּוֹר וָדוֹר חַיָּב אָדָם לִרְאוֹת אֶת־עַצְמוֹ כְּאִלּוּ הוּא יָצָא מִמִּצְרַיִם, שֶׁנֶּאֱמַר: וְהִגַּדְתָּ לְבִנְךָ בַּיּוֹם הַהוּא לֵאמֹר, בַּעֲבוּר זֶה עָשָׂה ה' לִי בְּצֵאתִי מִמִּצְרָיִם. לֹא אֶת־אֲבוֹתֵינוּ בִּלְבָד גָּאַל הַקָּדוֹשׁ בָּרוּךְ הוּא, אֶלָּא אַף אוֹתָנוּ גָּאַל עִמָּהֶם, שֶׁנֶּאֱמַר: וְאוֹתָנוּ הוֹצִיא מִשָּׁם, לְמַעַן הָבִיא אֹתָנוּ, לָתֶת לָנוּ אֶת־הָאָרֶץ אֲשֶׁר נִשְׁבַּע לַאֲבֹתֵינוּ.

In every generation a person is obligated to regard himself as if he had come out of Egypt

S2E2: The One With the Breastmilk
Monica: (Answering the phone) Hello? Oh, Hi, Ju-- Hi, Jew! Uh huh? Uh huh? Okay. Um, sure, that'd be great. See ya then. Bye.
Rachel: Did you just say "Hi, Jew?"
Monica: Yes. Uh, yes, I did. That was my friend, Eddie Moskowitz. Yeah, he likes it, reaffirms his faith.

FREEDOM. I WANT MY FREEDOM. [50]

The First Half of Hallel

He holds the cup in his hand and and he covers the matzah and says:

Therefore we are obligated to thank, praise, laud, glorify, exalt, lavish, bless, raise high, and acclaim He who made all these miracles for our ancestors and for us: He brought us out from slavery to freedom, from sorrow to joy, from mourning to [celebration of] a festival, from darkness to great light, and from servitude to redemption. And let us say a new song before Him, Halleluyah!

Halleluyah! Praise, servants of the Lord, praise the name of the Lord. May the Name of the Lord be blessed from now and forever. From the rising of the sun in the East to its setting, the name of the Lord is praised. Above all nations is the Lord, His honor is above the heavens.

חצי הלל

יאחז הכוס בידו ויכסה המצות ויאמר:

לְפִיכָךְ אֲנַחְנוּ חַיָּבִים לְהוֹדוֹת, לְהַלֵּל, לְשַׁבֵּחַ, לְפָאֵר, לְרוֹמֵם, לְהַדֵּר, לְבָרֵךְ, לְעַלֵּה וּלְקַלֵּס לְמִי שֶׁעָשָׂה לַאֲבוֹתֵינוּ וְלָנוּ אֶת־כָּל־הַנִּסִּים הָאֵלּוּ: הוֹצִיאָנוּ מֵעַבְדוּת לְחֵרוּת מִיָּגוֹן לְשִׂמְחָה, וּמֵאֵבֶל לְיוֹם טוֹב, וּמֵאֲפֵלָה לְאוֹר גָּדוֹל, וּמִשִּׁעְבּוּד לִגְאֻלָּה. וְנֹאמַר לְפָנָיו שִׁירָה חֲדָשָׁה: הַלְלוּיָהּ.

הַלְלוּיָהּ הַלְלוּ עַבְדֵי ה', הַלְלוּ אֶת־שֵׁם ה'. יְהִי שֵׁם ה' מְבֹרָךְ מֵעַתָּה וְעַד עוֹלָם. מִמִּזְרַח שֶׁמֶשׁ עַד מְבוֹאוֹ מְהֻלָּל שֵׁם ה'. רָם עַל־כָּל־גּוֹיִם ה', עַל הַשָּׁמַיִם כְּבוֹדוֹ.

Who is like the Lord, our God, Who sits on high; Who looks down upon the heavens and the earth? He brings up the poor out of the dirt; from the refuse piles, He raises the destitute. To seat him with the nobles, with the nobles of his people. He seats a barren woman in a home, a happy mother of children. Halleluyah!

In Israel's going out from Egypt, the house of Ya'akov from a people of foreign speech. Yehudah became His-holy one, Israel, His dominion. The Sea saw and fled, the Jordan turned to the rear. The mountains danced like rams, the hills like young sheep. What is happening to you, O Sea, that you are fleeing, O Jordan that you turn to the rear; O mountains that you dance like rams, O hills like young sheep? From before the Master, tremble O earth, from before the Lord of Ya'akov. He who turns the boulder into a pond of water, the flint into a spring of water.

מִי כַּיי אֱלֹהֵינוּ הַמַּגְבִּיהִי לָשָׁבֶת, הַמַּשְׁפִּילִי לִרְאוֹת בַּשָּׁמַיִם וּבָאָרֶץ? מְקִימִי מֵעָפָר דָּל, מֵאַשְׁפֹּת יָרִים אֶבְיוֹן, לְהוֹשִׁיבִי עִם-נְדִיבִים, עִם נְדִיבֵי עַמּוֹ. מוֹשִׁיבִי עֲקֶרֶת הַבַּיִת, אֵם הַבָּנִים שְׂמֵחָה. הַלְלוּיָהּ.

בְּצֵאת יִשְׂרָאֵל מִמִּצְרָיִם, בֵּית יַעֲקֹב מֵעַם לֹעֵז, הָיְתָה יְהוּדָה לְקָדְשׁוֹ, יִשְׂרָאֵל מַמְשְׁלוֹתָיו. הַיָּם רָאָה וַיָּנֹס, הַיַּרְדֵּן יִסֹּב לְאָחוֹר. הֶהָרִים רָקְדוּ כְאֵילִים, גְּבָעוֹת כִּבְנֵי צֹאן. מַה לְּךָ הַיָּם כִּי תָנוּס, הַיַּרְדֵּן – תִּסֹּב לְאָחוֹר, הֶהָרִים – תִּרְקְדוּ כְאֵילִים, גְּבָעוֹת כִּבְנֵי-צֹאן. מִלִּפְנֵי אָדוֹן חוּלִי אָרֶץ, מִלִּפְנֵי אֱלוֹהַּ יַעֲקֹב. הַהֹפְכִי הַצּוּר אֲגַם-מָיִם, חַלָּמִישׁ לְמַעְיְנוֹ-מָיִם.

S3E7 The One with the Race Car Bed
[Central Perk, the whole gang is there, Ross is telling a story about what happened at work and the rest of the gang are thinking to themselves, denoted by italics.]
Ross: So I told Carl, 'Nobody, no matter how famous their parents are, nobody is allowed to climb on the dinosaur.' But of course this went in one ear and out.....
(Everyone's thoughts start to wander.)
Rachel: *I love how he cares so much about stuff. If I squint I can pretend he's Alan Alda.*
Monica: *Oh good, another dinosaur story. When are those gonna become extinct?*
Chandler: *If I was a superhero who could fly and be invisible, that would be the best.*
Gunther: *What does Rachel see in this guy? I love Rachel. I wish she was my wife.*
Joey: *(singing in his head) dun da da dun dun dun da da dun*
Phoebe: Who's singing?

Second Cup of Wine

We raise the cup until we reach "who redeemed Israel".

Blessed are You, Lord our God, King of the universe, who redeemed us and redeemed our ancestors from Egypt, and brought us on this night to eat matzah and marror; so too, Lord our God, and God of our ancestors, bring us to other appointed times and holidays that will come to greet us in peace, joyful in the building of Your city and happy in Your worship; that we shall eat there from the offerings and from the Pesach sacrifices, the blood of which shall reach the wall of Your altar for favor, and we shall thank You with a new song upon our redemption and upon the restoration of our souls. Blessed are you, Lord, who redeemed Israel.

We say the blessing below and drink the cup while reclining to the left

Blessed are You, Lord our God, who creates the fruit of the vine.

כוס שניה

מגביהים את הכוס עד גאל ישראל.

בָּרוּךְ אַתָּה ה' אֱלֹהֵינוּ מֶלֶךְ הָעוֹלָם, אֲשֶׁר גְּאָלָנוּ וְגָאַל אֶת־אֲבוֹתֵינוּ מִמִּצְרַיִם, וְהִגִּיעָנוּ הַלַּיְלָה הַזֶּה לֶאֱכָל־בּוֹ מַצָּה וּמָרוֹר. כֵּן ה' אֱלֹהֵינוּ וֵאלֹהֵי אֲבוֹתֵינוּ יַגִּיעֵנוּ לְמוֹעֲדִים וְלִרְגָלִים אֲחֵרִים הַבָּאִים לִקְרָאתֵנוּ לְשָׁלוֹם, שְׂמֵחִים בְּבִנְיַן עִירֶךָ וְשָׂשִׂים בַּעֲבוֹדָתֶךָ. וְנֹאכַל שָׁם מִן הַזְּבָחִים וּמִן הַפְּסָחִים אֲשֶׁר יַגִּיעַ דָּמָם עַל קִיר מִזְבַּחֲךָ לְרָצוֹן, וְנוֹדֶה לְךָ שִׁיר חָדָשׁ עַל גְּאֻלָּתֵנוּ וְעַל פְּדוּת נַפְשֵׁנוּ. בָּרוּךְ אַתָּה ה', גָּאַל יִשְׂרָאֵל.

שותים את הכוס בהסבה שמאל.

בָּרוּךְ אַתָּה ה', אֱלֹהֵינוּ מֶלֶךְ הָעוֹלָם בּוֹרֵא פְּרִי הַגָּפֶן.

51

To conclude maggid...

S6E2: The One Where Ross Hugs Rachel
[At Central Perk, Phoebe is hosting an impromptu roundtable discussion with Stephanie, Karin, and Meg about Ross's three divorces.]
Ross: See, once you know the stories, it's not that bad....

First marriage, wife's hidden sexuality, not my fault.

Second marriage, said the wrong name at the alter, a little my fault.

Third marriage...well, they really shouldn't allow you to get married when you're that drunk and have writing all over your face, Nevada's fault.

RACHTZAH

Washing

We wash the hands and make the blessing.

Blessed are You, Lord our God, King of the Universe, who has sanctified us with His commandments and has commanded us on the washing of the hands.

רחצה

נוטלים את הידים ומברכים:

בָּרוּךְ אַתָּה ה׳, אֱלֹהֵינוּ מֶלֶךְ הָעוֹלָם, אֲשֶׁר קִדְּשָׁנוּ בְּמִצְוֹתָיו וְצִוָּנוּ עַל נְטִילַת יָדַיִם.

WASH YOUR HANDS![52] (with a bracha)

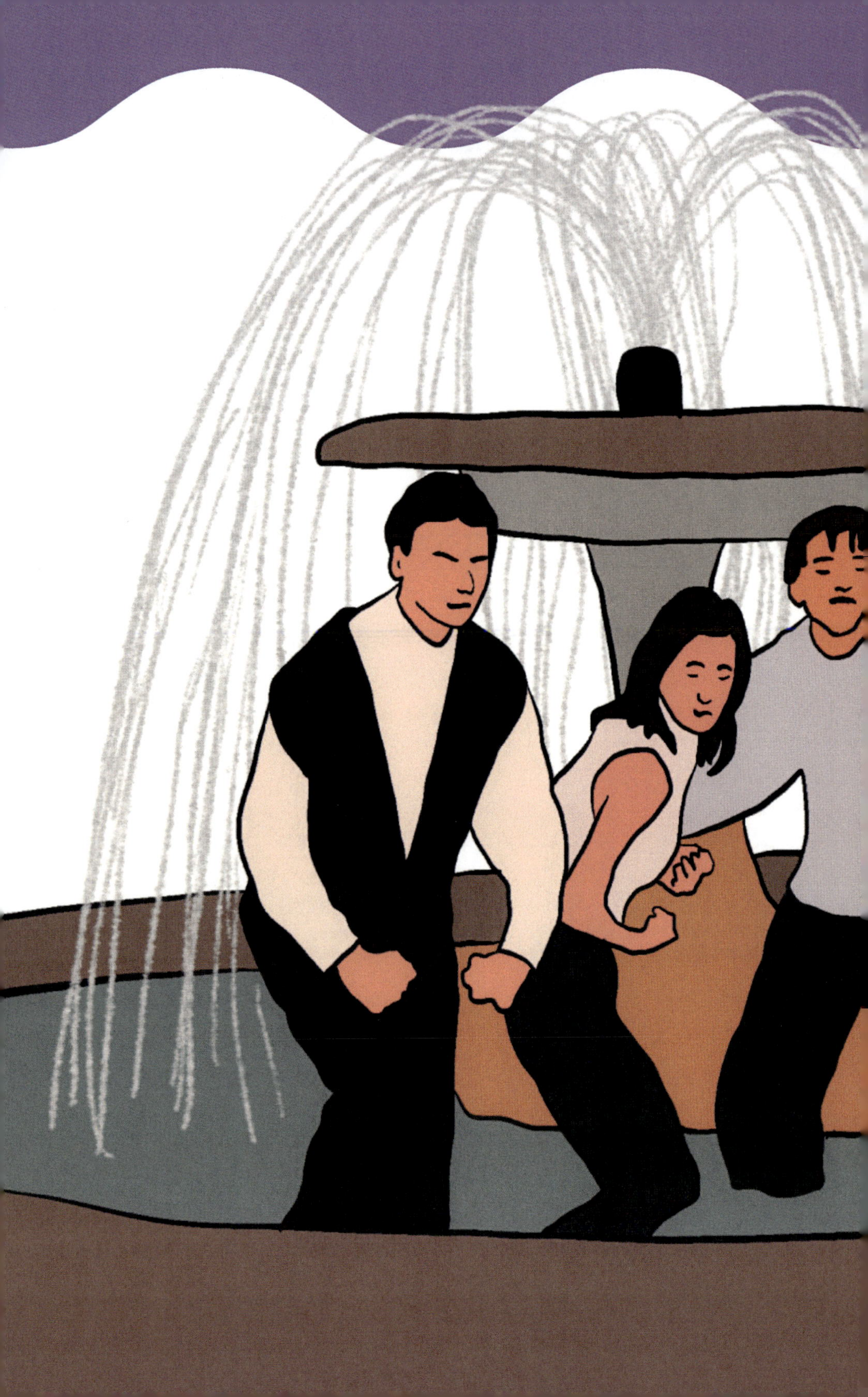

It is customary to bring a washing cup and basin for the head of the table to wash. Others just wash in the fountain.

MOTZI MATZAH

Motzi Matzah

He takes out the matzah in the order that he placed them, the broken one between the two whole ones; he holds the three of them in his hand and blesses "ha-motzi" with the intention to take from the top one and "on eating matzah" with the intention of eating from the broken one. Afterwards, he breaks off a kazayit from the top whole one and a second kazayit from the broken one and he dips them into salt and eats both while reclining.

Blessed are You, Lord our God, King of the Universe, who brings forth bread from the ground.

Blessed are You, Lord our God, King of the Universe, who has sanctified us with His commandments and has commanded us on the eating of matzah.

מוציא מצה

יקח המצות בסדר שהניחן, הפרוסה בין שתי השלמות, יאחז שלשתן בידו ויברך "המוציא" בכוונה על העליונה, ור"על אכילת מַצָּה" בכוונה על הפרוסה. אחר כך יבצע כזית מן העליונה השלמה וכזית שני מן הפרוסה, ויטבלם במלח, ויאכל בהסבה שני הזיתים:

בָּרוּךְ אַתָּה ה', אֱלֹהֵינוּ מֶלֶךְ הָעוֹלָם הַמּוֹצִיא לֶחֶם מִן הָאָרֶץ.

בָּרוּךְ אַתָּה ה', אֱלֹהֵינוּ מֶלֶךְ הָעוֹלָם, אֲשֶׁר קִדְּשָׁנוּ בְּמִצְוֹתָיו וְצִוָּנוּ עַל אֲכִילַת מַצָּה.

Remember to eat the matzot in a reclining position.

MAROR

Marror

All present should take a kazayit of marror, dip into the haroset, shake off the haroset, make the blessing and eat without reclining.

Blessed are You, Lord our God, King of the Universe, who has sanctified us with His commandments and has commanded us on the eating of marror.

מרור

כל אחד מהמסבים לוקח כזית מרור, מטבלו בחרוסת, מנער החרוסת, מברך ואוכל בלי הסבה.

בָּרוּךְ אַתָּה ה׳, אֱלֹהֵינוּ מֶלֶךְ הָעוֹלָם, אֲשֶׁר קִדְּשָׁנוּ בְּמִצְוֹתָיו וְצִוָּנוּ עַל אֲכִילַת מָרוֹר.

S2E14: The One With the Prom Video
Restaurant Manager: All right. Let's see if you're as good in person as you are on paper. Make me a salad.
Monica: A salad? Really, I could do something more complicated if you like.
Manager: No, just the salad will be fine.
Monica: Okay, you got it.
Manager: Now I want you to tell me what you're doing while you're doing it.
Monica: All right. Well, I'm tearing the lettuce.
Restaurant Manager: Uh-huh. Is it dirty?
Monica: Oh, no, don't worry. I'm gonna wash it.
Manager: Don't. I like it dirty.
Monica: That's your call.

Monica: You had a salad.
Phoebe: No wonder I don't feel full.[54]

KORECH

Wrap

כורך

All present should take a kazayit from the third whole matzah with a kazayit of marror, wrap them together and eat them while reclining and without saying a blessing. Before he eats it, he should say:

כל אחד מהמסבים לוקח כזית מן המצה השלישית עם כזית מרור, כורכים יחד, אוכלים בהסבה ובלי ברכה. לפני אכלו אומר.

In memory of the Temple according to Hillel. This is what Hillel would do when the Temple existed:

זֵכֶר לְמִקְדָּשׁ כְּהִלֵּל. כֵּן עָשָׂה הִלֵּל בִּזְמַן שֶׁבֵּית הַמִּקְדָּשׁ הָיָה קַיָּם:

He would wrap the matzah and marror and eat them together, in order to fulfill what is stated: "You should eat it upon matzot and marrorim."

הָיָה כּוֹרֵךְ מַצָּה וּמָרוֹר וְאוֹכֵל בְּיַחַד, לְקַיֵּם מַה שֶּׁנֶּאֱמַר: עַל מַצּוֹת וּמְרוֹרִים יֹאכְלֻהוּ.

If Ross would have created the Korech Sandwich:

Someone at work ate my sandwich!

Well, what did the police say?[55]

That sandwich was the only good thing in my life!⁵⁶

You - you ate my sandwich? MY SANDWICH?!⁵⁷

Knock Knock, who's there?
Ross Geller's lunch.
Ross Geller's lunch who?
Ross Geller's lunch please dont take me, ok?

I call it "The Moist-Maker"⁵⁸

SHULCHAN ORECH

The Set Table

We eat and drink.

שלחן עורך

אוכלים ושותים.

Side Dish:

Salmon skin roll.⁶⁰

Unagi!

S7E16: The One with the Truth About London
Joey: What's my little chef got for me tonight?
Monica: Your favorite!
Joey: Ho-ho-ho, fried stuff with cheese!

Main Course:

Okay, I've got a leg, three breasts, and a wing.

Well, how do you find clothes that fit?⁶¹

S8E9: The One With the Rumor
Phoebe: Joey, those are my maternity pants!
Joey: No, these are my **PASSOVER** pants!

TZAFUN

The Concealed [Matzah]

צפון

After the end of the meal, all those present take a kazayit from the matzah, that was concealed for the afikoman, and eat a kazayit from it while reclining.

אחר גמר הסעודה לוקח כל אחד מהמסבים כזית מהמצה שהייתה צפונה לאפיקומן ואוכל ממנה כזית בהסבה. וצריך לאוכלה קודם חצות הלילה.

Before eating the afikoman, he should say: **"In memory of the Pesach sacrifice that was eaten upon being satiated."**

לפני אכילת האפיקומן יאמר:
זֵכֶר לְקָרְבַּן פֶּסַח הַנֶּאֱכָל עַל הַשּׂוֹבַע.

Time to find the Afikomen!

Joey: Where did you have it last?
Phoebe: Duy! Probably right before she lost it.

You don't get a lot of "duy" these days.[62]

S6E10: The One with the Routine
Phoebe: Ooh, who's it for?
Rachel: "Dear losers, do you really think I'd hide presents under the couch? P.S., Chandler, I knew they'd break you."

Phoebe: Hey! I got you a present!
Chandler: Oh, my goodness, where did you hide it?[63]

Dessert Time...

S6E9: The One Where Ross Got High
Rachel: It's a trifle. It's got all of these layers. First, there's a layer of ladyfingers, then a layer of jam, then custard, which I made from scratch. Raspberries, more ladyfingers...Then beef sautéed with peas and onions. Then more custard and then bananas and then I just put some whipped cream on top.

BARECH

Bless

We pour the third cup and recite the Grace After the Meal.

A Song of Ascents; When the Lord will bring back the captivity of Zion, we will be like dreamers. Then our mouth will be full of mirth and our tongue joyful melody; then they will say among the nations; "The Lord has done greatly with these." The Lord has done great things with us; we are happy. Lord, return our captivity like streams in the desert. Those that sow with tears will reap with joyful song. He who surely goes and cries, he carries the measure of seed, he will surely come in joyful song and carry his sheaves.

ברך

מוזגים כוס שלישי ומברכים ברכת המזון.

שִׁיר הַמַּעֲלוֹת, בְּשׁוּב ה' אֶת שִׁיבַת צִיּוֹן הָיִינוּ כְּחֹלְמִים. אָז יִמָּלֵא שְׂחוֹק פִּינוּ וּלְשׁוֹנֵנוּ רִנָּה. אָז יֹאמְרוּ בַגּוֹיִם: הִגְדִּיל ה' לַעֲשׂוֹת עִם אֵלֶּה. הִגְדִּיל ה' לַעֲשׂוֹת עִמָּנוּ, הָיִינוּ שְׂמֵחִים. שׁוּבָה ה' אֶת שְׁבִיתֵנוּ כַּאֲפִיקִים בַּנֶּגֶב. הַזֹּרְעִים בְּדִמְעָה, בְּרִנָּה יִקְצֹרוּ. הָלוֹךְ יֵלֵךְ וּבָכֹה נֹשֵׂא מֶשֶׁךְ הַזָּרַע, בֹּא יָבֹא בְרִנָּה נֹשֵׂא אֲלֻמֹּתָיו.

Three that ate together are obligated to introduce the blessing and the leader of the introduction opens as follows:	שלשה שֶׁאָכְלוּ כְּאֶחָד חַיָּבִים לְזַמֵּן וְהַמְזַמֵּן פּוֹתֵחַ:
My masters, let us bless:	רַבּוֹתַי נְבָרֵךְ:
All those present answer:	הַמְסֻבִּים עוֹנִים:
May the Name of the Lord be blessed from now and forever.	יְהִי שֵׁם ה' מְבֹרָךְ מֵעַתָּה וְעַד עוֹלָם.
The leader says:	הַמְזַמֵּן אוֹמֵר:
With the permission of our gentlemen and our teachers and my masters, let us bless [our God] from whom we have eaten.	בִּרְשׁוּת מָרָנָן וְרַבָּנָן וְרַבּוֹתַי, נְבָרֵךְ [אֱלֹהֵינוּ] שֶׁאָכַלְנוּ מִשֶּׁלּוֹ.
Those present answer:	הַמְסֻבִּים עוֹנִים:
Blessed is [our God] from whom we have eaten and from whose goodness we live.	בָּרוּךְ [אֱלֹהֵינוּ] שֶׁאָכַלְנוּ מִשֶּׁלּוֹ וּבְטוּבוֹ חָיִינוּ
The leader repeats and says:	הַמְזַמֵּן חוֹזֵר וְאוֹמֵר:
Blessed is [our God] from whom we have eaten and from whose goodness we live.	בָּרוּךְ [אֱלֹהֵינוּ] שֶׁאָכַלְנוּ מִשֶּׁלּוֹ וּבְטוּבוֹ חָיִינוּ
They all say:	כֻּלָּם אוֹמְרִים:

Blessed are You, Lord our God, King of the Universe, who nourishes the entire world in His goodness, in grace, in kindness and in mercy; He gives bread to all flesh since His kindness is forever. And in His great goodness, we always have not lacked, and may we not lack nourishment forever and always, because of His great name. Since He is a Power that feeds and provides for all and does good to all and prepares nourishment for all of his creatures that he created. Blessed are You, Lord, who sustains all.

בָּרוּךְ אַתָּה ה', אֱלֹהֵינוּ מֶלֶךְ הָעוֹלָם, הַזָּן אֶת הָעוֹלָם כֻּלּוֹ בְּטוּבוֹ בְּחֵן בְּחֶסֶד וּבְרַחֲמִים, הוּא נוֹתֵן לֶחֶם לְכָל בָּשָׂר כִּי לְעוֹלָם חַסְדּוֹ. וּבְטוּבוֹ הַגָּדוֹל תָּמִיד לֹא חָסַר לָנוּ, וְאַל יֶחְסַר לָנוּ מָזוֹן לְעוֹלָם וָעֶד. בַּעֲבוּר שְׁמוֹ הַגָּדוֹל, כִּי הוּא אֵל זָן וּמְפַרְנֵס לַכֹּל וּמֵטִיב לַכֹּל, וּמֵכִין מָזוֹן לְכָל בְּרִיּוֹתָיו אֲשֶׁר בָּרָא. בָּרוּךְ אַתָּה ה', הַזָּן אֶת הַכֹּל.

נוֹדֶה לְךָ ה' אֱלֹהֵינוּ עַל שֶׁהִנְחַלְתָּ לַאֲבוֹתֵינוּ אֶרֶץ חֶמְדָּה טוֹבָה וּרְחָבָה, וְעַל שֶׁהוֹצֵאתָנוּ ה' אֱלֹהֵינוּ מֵאֶרֶץ מִצְרַיִם, וּפְדִיתָנוּ מִבֵּית עֲבָדִים, וְעַל בְּרִיתְךָ שֶׁחָתַמְתָּ בִּבְשָׂרֵנוּ, וְעַל תּוֹרָתְךָ שֶׁלִּמַּדְתָּנוּ, וְעַל חֻקֶּיךָ שֶׁהוֹדַעְתָּנוּ, וְעַל חַיִּים חֵן וָחֶסֶד שֶׁחוֹנַנְתָּנוּ, וְעַל אֲכִילַת מָזוֹן שָׁאַתָּה זָן וּמְפַרְנֵס אוֹתָנוּ תָּמִיד, בְּכָל יוֹם וּבְכָל עֵת וּבְכָל שָׁעָה:

וְעַל הַכֹּל ה' אֱלֹהֵינוּ, אֲנַחְנוּ מוֹדִים לָךְ וּמְבָרְכִים אוֹתָךְ, יִתְבָּרַךְ שִׁמְךָ בְּפִי כָּל חַי תָּמִיד לְעוֹלָם וָעֶד. כַּכָּתוּב: וְאָכַלְתָּ וְשָׂבָעְתָּ וּבֵרַכְתָּ אֶת ה' אֱלֹהֶיךָ עַל הָאָרֶץ הַטּוֹבָה אֲשֶׁר נָתַן לָךְ. בָּרוּךְ אַתָּה ה', עַל הָאָרֶץ וְעַל הַמָּזוֹן:

רַחֶם נָא ה' אֱלֹהֵינוּ עַל יִשְׂרָאֵל עַמֶּךָ וְעַל יְרוּשָׁלַיִם עִירֶךָ וְעַל צִיּוֹן מִשְׁכַּן כְּבוֹדֶךָ וְעַל מַלְכוּת בֵּית דָּוִד מְשִׁיחֶךָ וְעַל הַבַּיִת הַגָּדוֹל וְהַקָּדוֹשׁ שֶׁנִּקְרָא שִׁמְךָ עָלָיו: אֱלֹהֵינוּ אָבִינוּ, רְעֵנוּ זוּנֵנוּ פַּרְנְסֵנוּ וְכַלְכְּלֵנוּ וְהַרְוִיחֵנוּ, וְהַרְוַח לָנוּ ה' אֱלֹהֵינוּ מְהֵרָה מִכָּל צָרוֹתֵינוּ. וְנָא אַל תַּצְרִיכֵנוּ ה' אֱלֹהֵינוּ, לֹא לִידֵי מַתְּנַת בָּשָׂר וָדָם וְלֹא לִידֵי הַלְוָאָתָם, כִּי אִם לְיָדְךָ הַמְּלֵאָה הַפְּתוּחָה הַקְּדוֹשָׁה וְהָרְחָבָה, שֶׁלֹּא נֵבוֹשׁ וְלֹא נִכָּלֵם לְעוֹלָם וָעֶד.

We thank you, Lord our God, that you have given as an inheritance to our ancestors a lovely, good and broad land, and that You took us out, Lord our God, from the land of Egypt and that You redeemed us from a house of slaves, and for Your covenant which You have sealed in our flesh, and for Your Torah that You have taught us, and for Your statutes which You have made known to us, and for life, grace and kindness that You have granted us and for the eating of nourishment that You feed and provide for us always, on all days, and at all times and in every hour.

And for everything, Lord our God, we thank You and bless You; may Your name be blessed by the mouth of all life, constantly forever and always, as it is written (Deuteronomy 8:10); "And you shall eat and you shall be satiated and you shall bless the Lord your God for the good land that He has given you." Blessed are You, Lord, for the land and for the nourishment.

Please have mercy, Lord our God, upon Israel, Your people; and upon Jerusalem, Your city; and upon Zion, the dwelling place of Your Glory; and upon the monarchy of the House of David, Your appointed one; and upon the great and holy house that Your name is called upon. Our God, our Father, tend us, sustain us, provide for us, relieve us and give us quick relief, Lord our God, from all of our troubles. And please do not make us needy, Lord our God, not for the gifts of flesh and blood, and not for their loans, but rather from Your full, open, holy and broad hand, so that we not be embarrassed and we not be ashamed forever and always.

בשבת מוסיפין:

On Shabbat, we add the following paragraph.

רְצֵה וְהַחֲלִיצֵנוּ ה' אֱלֹהֵינוּ בְּמִצְוֹתֶיךָ וּבְמִצְוַת יוֹם הַשְּׁבִיעִי הַשַּׁבָּת הַגָּדוֹל וְהַקָּדוֹשׁ הַזֶּה. כִּי יוֹם זֶה גָּדוֹל וְקָדוֹשׁ הוּא לְפָנֶיךָ לִשְׁבָּת בּוֹ וְלָנוּחַ בּוֹ בְּאַהֲבָה כְּמִצְוַת רְצוֹנֶךָ. וּבִרְצוֹנְךָ הָנִיחַ לָנוּ ה' אֱלֹהֵינוּ שֶׁלֹּא תְהֵא צָרָה וְיָגוֹן וַאֲנָחָה בְּיוֹם מְנוּחָתֵנוּ. וְהַרְאֵנוּ ה' אֱלֹהֵינוּ בְּנֶחָמַת צִיּוֹן עִירֶךָ וּבְבִנְיַן יְרוּשָׁלַיִם עִיר קָדְשֶׁךָ כִּי אַתָּה הוּא בַּעַל הַיְשׁוּעוֹת וּבַעַל הַנֶּחָמוֹת.

May You be pleased to embolden us, Lord our God, in your commandments and in the command of the seventh day, of this great and holy Shabbat, since this day is great and holy before You, to cease work upon it and to rest upon it, with love, according to the commandment of Your will. And with Your will, allow us, Lord our God, that we should not have trouble, and grief and sighing on the day of our rest. And may You show us, Lord our God, the consolation of Zion, Your city; and the building of Jerusalem, Your holy city; since You are the Master of salvations and the Master of consolations.

אֱלֹהֵינוּ וֵאלֹהֵי אֲבוֹתֵינוּ, יַעֲלֶה וְיָבֹא וְיַגִּיעַ וְיֵרָאֶה וְיֵרָצֶה וְיִשָּׁמַע וְיִפָּקֵד וְיִזָּכֵר זִכְרוֹנֵנוּ וּפִקְדוֹנֵנוּ, וְזִכְרוֹן אֲבוֹתֵינוּ, וְזִכְרוֹן מָשִׁיחַ בֶּן דָּוִד עַבְדֶּךָ, וְזִכְרוֹן יְרוּשָׁלַיִם עִיר קָדְשֶׁךָ, וְזִכְרוֹן כָּל עַמְּךָ בֵּית יִשְׂרָאֵל לְפָנֶיךָ, לִפְלֵיטָה לְטוֹבָה לְחֵן וּלְחֶסֶד וּלְרַחֲמִים, לְחַיִּים וּלְשָׁלוֹם בְּיוֹם חַג הַמַּצּוֹת הַזֶּה זָכְרֵנוּ ה' אֱלֹהֵינוּ בּוֹ לְטוֹבָה וּפָקְדֵנוּ בוֹ לִבְרָכָה וְהוֹשִׁיעֵנוּ בוֹ לְחַיִּים. וּבִדְבַר יְשׁוּעָה וְרַחֲמִים חוּס וְחָנֵּנוּ וְרַחֵם עָלֵינוּ וְהוֹשִׁיעֵנוּ, כִּי אֵלֶיךָ עֵינֵינוּ, כִּי אֵל מֶלֶךְ חַנּוּן וְרַחוּם אָתָּה. וּבְנֵה יְרוּשָׁלַיִם עִיר הַקֹּדֶשׁ בִּמְהֵרָה בְיָמֵינוּ. בָּרוּךְ אַתָּה ה', בּוֹנֵה בְרַחֲמָיו יְרוּשָׁלָיִם. אָמֵן.

God and God of our ancestors, may there ascend and come and reach and be seen and be acceptable and be heard and be recalled and be remembered - our remembrance and our recollection; and the remembrance of our ancestors; and the remembrance of the messiah, the son of David, Your servant; and the remembrance of Jerusalem, Your holy city; and the remembrance of all Your people, the house of Israel - in front of You, for survival, for good, for grace, and for kindness, and for mercy, for life and for peace on this day of the Festival of matzot. Remember us, Lord our God, on it for good and recall us on it for survival and save us on it for life, and by the word of salvation and mercy, pity and grace us and have mercy on us and save us, since our eyes are upon You, since You are a graceful and merciful Power. And may You build Jerusalem, the holy city, quickly and in our days. Blessed are You, Lord, who builds Jerusalem in His mercy. Amen.

Blessed are You, Lord our God, King of the Universe, the Power, our Father, our King, our Mighty One, our Creator, our Redeemer, our Shaper, our Holy One, the Holy One of Ya'akov, our Shepard, the Shepard of Israel, the good King, who does good to all, since on every single day He has done good, He does good, He will do good, to us; He has granted us, He grants us, He will grant us forever - in grace and in kindness, and in mercy, and in relief - rescue and success, blessing and salvation, consolation, provision and relief and mercy and life and peace and all good; and may we not lack any good ever.

May the Merciful One reign over us forever and always. May the Merciful One be blessed in the heavens and in the earth. May the Merciful One be praised for all generations, and exalted among us forever and ever, and glorified among us always and infinitely for all infinities. May the Merciful One sustain us honorably. May the Merciful One break our yolk from upon our necks and bring us upright to our land. May the Merciful One send us multiple blessing, to this home and upon this table upon which we have eaten. May the Merciful One send us Eliyahu the prophet - may he be remembered for good - and he shall announce to us tidings of good, of salvation and of consolation. May the Merciful One bless my husband/my wife. May the Merciful One bless [my father, my teacher,] the master of this home and [my mother, my teacher,] the mistress of this home, they and their home and their offspring and everything that is theirs. Us and all that is ours; as were blessed Avraham, Yitschak and Ya'akov, in everything, from everything, with everything, so too should He bless us, all of us together, with a complete blessing and we shall say, Amen.

בָּרוּךְ אַתָּה ה', אֱלֹהֵינוּ מֶלֶךְ הָעוֹלָם, הָאֵל אָבִינוּ מַלְכֵּנוּ אַדִּירֵנוּ בּוֹרְאֵנוּ גּוֹאֲלֵנוּ יוֹצְרֵנוּ קְדוֹשֵׁנוּ קְדוֹשׁ יַעֲקֹב רוֹעֵנוּ רוֹעֵה יִשְׂרָאֵל הַמֶּלֶךְ הַטּוֹב וְהַמֵּטִיב לַכֹּל שֶׁבְּכָל יוֹם וָיוֹם הוּא הֵטִיב, הוּא מֵטִיב, הוּא יֵיטִיב לָנוּ. הוּא גְמָלָנוּ הוּא גוֹמְלֵנוּ הוּא יִגְמְלֵנוּ לָעַד, לְחֵן וּלְחֶסֶד וּלְרַחֲמִים וּלְרֶוַח הַצָּלָה וְהַצְלָחָה, בְּרָכָה וִישׁוּעָה נֶחָמָה פַּרְנָסָה וְכַלְכָּלָה וְרַחֲמִים וְחַיִּים וְשָׁלוֹם וְכָל טוֹב, וּמִכָּל טוּב לְעוֹלָם עַל יְחַסְּרֵנוּ.

הָרַחֲמָן הוּא יִמְלוֹךְ עָלֵינוּ לְעוֹלָם וָעֶד. הָרַחֲמָן הוּא יִתְבָּרַךְ בַּשָּׁמַיִם וּבָאָרֶץ. הָרַחֲמָן הוּא יִשְׁתַּבַּח לְדוֹר דּוֹרִים, וְיִתְפָּאַר בָּנוּ לָעַד וּלְנֵצַח נְצָחִים, וְיִתְהַדַּר בָּנוּ לָעַד וּלְעוֹלְמֵי עוֹלָמִים. הָרַחֲמָן הוּא יְפַרְנְסֵנוּ בְּכָבוֹד. הָרַחֲמָן הוּא יִשְׁבּוֹר עֻלֵּנוּ מֵעַל צַוָּארֵנוּ, וְהוּא יוֹלִיכֵנוּ קוֹמְמִיּוּת לְאַרְצֵנוּ. הָרַחֲמָן הוּא יִשְׁלַח לָנוּ בְּרָכָה מְרֻבָּה בַּבַּיִת הַזֶּה, וְעַל שֻׁלְחָן זֶה שֶׁאָכַלְנוּ עָלָיו. הָרַחֲמָן הוּא יִשְׁלַח לָנוּ אֶת אֵלִיָּהוּ הַנָּבִיא זָכוּר לַטּוֹב, וִיבַשֶּׂר לָנוּ בְּשׂוֹרוֹת טוֹבוֹת יְשׁוּעוֹת וְנֶחָמוֹת. הָרַחֲמָן הוּא יְבָרֵךְ אֶת בַּעֲלִי / אִשְׁתִּי. הָרַחֲמָן הוּא יְבָרֵךְ אֶת [אָבִי מוֹרִי] בַּעַל הַבַּיִת הַזֶּה. וְאֶת [אִמִּי מוֹרָתִי] בַּעֲלַת הַבַּיִת הַזֶּה, אוֹתָם וְאֶת בֵּיתָם וְאֶת זַרְעָם וְאֶת כָּל אֲשֶׁר לָהֶם. אוֹתָנוּ וְאֶת כָּל אֲשֶׁר לָנוּ, כְּמוֹ שֶׁנִּתְבָּרְכוּ אֲבוֹתֵינוּ אַבְרָהָם יִצְחָק וְיַעֲקֹב בַּכֹּל מִכֹּל כֹּל, כֵּן יְבָרֵךְ אוֹתָנוּ כֻּלָּנוּ יַחַד בִּבְרָכָה שְׁלֵמָה, וְנֹאמַר, אָמֵן.

בַּמָּרוֹם יְלַמְּדוּ עֲלֵיהֶם וְעָלֵינוּ זְכוּת שֶׁתְּהֵא לְמִשְׁמֶרֶת שָׁלוֹם. וְנִשָּׂא בְרָכָה מֵאֵת ה', וּצְדָקָה מֵאֱלֹהֵי יִשְׁעֵנוּ, וְנִמְצָא חֵן וְשֵׂכֶל טוֹב בְּעֵינֵי אֱלֹהִים וְאָדָם. בשבת: הָרַחֲמָן הוּא יַנְחִילֵנוּ יוֹם שֶׁכֻּלוֹ שַׁבָּת וּמְנוּחָה לְחַיֵּי הָעוֹלָמִים. הָרַחֲמָן הוּא יַנְחִילֵנוּ יוֹם שֶׁכֻּלוֹ טוֹב.[יוֹם שֶׁכֻּלוֹ אָרוּךְ. יוֹם שֶׁצַּדִּיקִים יוֹשְׁבִים וְעַטְרוֹתֵיהֶם בְּרָאשֵׁיהֶם וְנֶהֱנִים מִזִּיו הַשְּׁכִינָה וִיהִי חֶלְקֵינוּ עִמָּהֶם]. הָרַחֲמָן הוּא יְזַכֵּנוּ לִימוֹת הַמָּשִׁיחַ וּלְחַיֵּי הָעוֹלָם הַבָּא. מִגְדּוֹל יְשׁוּעוֹת מַלְכּוֹ וְעֹשֶׂה חֶסֶד לִמְשִׁיחוֹ לְדָוִד וּלְזַרְעוֹ עַד עוֹלָם. עֹשֶׂה שָׁלוֹם בִּמְרוֹמָיו, הוּא יַעֲשֶׂה שָׁלוֹם עָלֵינוּ וְעַל כָּל יִשְׂרָאֵל וְאִמְרוּ, אָמֵן.

יְראוּ אֶת ה' קְדֹשָׁיו, כִּי אֵין מַחְסוֹר לִירֵאָיו. כְּפִירִים רָשׁוּ וְרָעֵבוּ, וְדֹרְשֵׁי ה' לֹא יַחְסְרוּ כָל טוֹב. הוֹדוּ לַיי כִּי טוֹב כִּי לְעוֹלָם חַסְדּוֹ. פּוֹתֵחַ אֶת יָדֶךָ, וּמַשְׂבִּיעַ לְכָל חַי רָצוֹן. בָּרוּךְ הַגֶּבֶר אֲשֶׁר יִבְטַח בַּיי, וְהָיָה ה' מִבְטַחוֹ. נַעַר הָיִיתִי גַם זָקַנְתִּי, וְלֹא רָאִיתִי צַדִּיק נֶעֱזָב, וְזַרְעוֹ מְבַקֶּשׁ לָחֶם. יי עֹז לְעַמּוֹ יִתֵּן, ה' יְבָרֵךְ אֶת עַמּוֹ בַשָּׁלוֹם.

From above, may they advocate upon them and upon us merit, that should protect us in peace; and may we carry a blessing from the Lord and charity from the God of our salvation; and find grace and good understanding in the eyes of God and man. [On Shabbat, we say: May the Merciful One give us to inherit the day that will be completely Shabbat and rest in everlasting life.] May the Merciful One give us to inherit the day that will be all good. [The day that is all long, the day that the righteous will sit and their crowns will be on their heads and they will enjoy the radiance of the Divine presence and my our share be with them.] May the Merciful One give us merit for the times of the messiah and for life in the world to come. A tower of salvations is our King; may He do kindness with his messiah, with David and his offspring, forever. The One who makes peace above, may He make peace upon us and upon all of Israel; and say, Amen.

Fear the Lord, His holy ones, since there is no lacking for those that fear Him. Young lions may go without and hunger, but those that seek the Lord will not lack any good thing. Thank the Lord, since He is good, since His kindness is forever. You open Your hand and satisfy the will of all living things. Blessed is the man that trusts in the Lord and the Lord is his security. I was a youth and I have also aged and I have not seen a righteous man forsaken and his offspring seeking bread. The Lord will give courage to His people. The Lord will bless His people with peace.

Third Cup of Wine

Blessed are You, Lord our God, King of the universe, who creates the fruit of the vine.

We drink while reclining and do not say a blessing afterwards.

כוס שלישית

בָּרוּךְ אַתָּה ה׳, אֱלֹהֵינוּ מֶלֶךְ הָעוֹלָם בּוֹרֵא פְּרִי הַגָּפֶן.

ושותים בהסיבה ואינו מברך ברכה אחרונה.

S6E1: The One After Vegas
Phoebe: I'm so drunk right now! What, I can't have a mimosa with breakfast? I'm on vacation!

I'M SO DRUNK!

Pour Out Thy Wrath

We pour the cup of Eliyahu and open the door.

Pour your wrath upon the nations that did not know You and upon the kingdoms that did not call upon Your Name! Since they have consumed Ya'akov and laid waste his habitation. Pour out Your fury upon them and the fierceness of Your anger shall reach them! You shall pursue them with anger and eradicate them from under the skies of the Lord.

שפך חמתך

מוזגים כוס של אליהו ופותחים את הדלת:

שְׁפֹךְ חֲמָתְךָ אֶל־הַגּוֹיִם אֲשֶׁר לֹא יְדָעוּךָ וְעַל־מַמְלָכוֹת אֲשֶׁר בְּשִׁמְךָ לֹא קָרָאוּ. כִּי אָכַל אֶת־יַעֲקֹב וְאֶת־נָוֵהוּ הֵשַׁמּוּ. שְׁפָךְ־עֲלֵיהֶם זַעְמֶךָ וַחֲרוֹן אַפְּךָ יַשִּׂיגֵם. תִּרְדֹּף בְּאַף וְתַשְׁמִידֵם מִתַּחַת שְׁמֵי ה'.

HALLEL

Hallel

We pour the fourth cup and complete the Hallel.

Not to us, not to us, but rather to Your name, give glory for your kindness and for your truth. Why should the nations say, "Say, where is their God?" But our God is in the heavens, all that He wanted, He has done. Their idols are silver and gold, the work of men's hands. They have a mouth but do not speak; they have eyes but do not see. They have ears but do not hear; they have a nose but do not smell. Hands, but they do not feel; feet, but do not walk; they do not make a peep from their throat. Like them will be their makers, all those that trust in them. Israel, trust in the Lord; their help and shield is He. House of Aharon, trust in the Lord; their help and shield is He. Those that fear the Lord, trust in the Lord; their help and shield is He. The Lord who remembers us, will bless;

הלל

מוזגין כוס רביעי וגומרין עליו את ההלל.

לֹא לָנוּ, ה׳, לֹא לָנוּ, כִּי לְשִׁמְךָ תֵּן כָּבוֹד, עַל חַסְדְּךָ עַל אֲמִתֶּךָ. לָמָּה יֹאמְרוּ הַגּוֹיִם אַיֵּה נָא אֱלֹהֵיהֶם. וֵאלֹהֵינוּ בַשָּׁמַיִם, כֹּל אֲשֶׁר חָפֵץ עָשָׂה. עֲצַבֵּיהֶם כֶּסֶף וְזָהָב מַעֲשֵׂה יְדֵי אָדָם. פֶּה לָהֶם וְלֹא יְדַבֵּרוּ, עֵינַיִם לָהֶם וְלֹא יִרְאוּ. אָזְנַיִם לָהֶם וְלֹא יִשְׁמָעוּ, אַף לָהֶם וְלֹא יְרִיחוּן. יְדֵיהֶם וְלֹא יְמִישׁוּן, רַגְלֵיהֶם וְלֹא יְהַלֵּכוּ, לֹא יֶהְגּוּ בִּגְרוֹנָם. כְּמוֹהֶם יִהְיוּ עֹשֵׂיהֶם, כֹּל אֲשֶׁר בֹּטֵחַ בָּהֶם. יִשְׂרָאֵל בְּטַח בַּיי, עֶזְרָם וּמָגִנָּם הוּא. בֵּית אַהֲרֹן בִּטְחוּ בַיי, עֶזְרָם וּמָגִנָּם הוּא. יִרְאֵי ה׳ בִּטְחוּ בַיי, עֶזְרָם וּמָגִנָּם הוּא. יי זְכָרָנוּ יְבָרֵךְ.

יְבָרֵךְ אֶת בֵּית יִשְׂרָאֵל, יְבָרֵךְ אֶת בֵּית אַהֲרֹן, יְבָרֵךְ יִרְאֵי ה', הַקְּטַנִּים עִם הַגְּדֹלִים. יֹסֵף ה' עֲלֵיכֶם, עֲלֵיכֶם וְעַל בְּנֵיכֶם. בְּרוּכִים אַתֶּם לַיי, עֹשֵׂה שָׁמַיִם וָאָרֶץ. הַשָּׁמַיִם שָׁמַיִם לַיי וְהָאָרֶץ נָתַן לִבְנֵי אָדָם. לֹא הַמֵּתִים יְהַלְלוּ יָהּ וְלֹא כָּל יֹרְדֵי דוּמָה. וַאֲנַחְנוּ נְבָרֵךְ יָהּ מֵעַתָּה וְעַד עוֹלָם. הַלְלוּיָהּ.

He will bless the House of Israel; He will bless the House of Aharon. He will bless those that fear the Lord, the small ones with the great ones. May the Lord bring increase to you, to you and to your children. Blessed are you to the Lord, the maker of the heavens and the earth. The heavens, are the Lord's heavens, but the earth He has given to the children of man. It is not the dead that will praise the Lord, and not those that go down to silence. But we will bless the Lord from now and forever. Halleluyah!

אָהַבְתִּי כִּי יִשְׁמַע ה' אֶת קוֹלִי תַּחֲנוּנָי. כִּי הִטָּה אָזְנוֹ לִי וּבְיָמַי אֶקְרָא. אֲפָפוּנִי חֶבְלֵי מָוֶת וּמְצָרֵי שְׁאוֹל מְצָאוּנִי, צָרָה וְיָגוֹן אֶמְצָא. וּבְשֵׁם ה' אֶקְרָא: אָנָּא ה' מַלְּטָה נַפְשִׁי. חַנּוּן ה' וְצַדִּיק, וֵאלֹהֵינוּ מְרַחֵם. שֹׁמֵר פְּתָאיִם ה', דַּלּוֹתִי וְלִי יְהוֹשִׁיעַ. שׁוּבִי נַפְשִׁי לִמְנוּחָיְכִי, כִּי ה' גָּמַל עָלָיְכִי. כִּי חִלַּצְתָּ נַפְשִׁי מִמָּוֶת, אֶת עֵינִי מִן דִּמְעָה, אֶת רַגְלִי מִדֶּחִי. אֶתְהַלֵּךְ לִפְנֵי ה' בְּאַרְצוֹת הַחַיִּים. הֶאֱמַנְתִּי כִּי אֲדַבֵּר, אֲנִי עָנִיתִי מְאֹד. אֲנִי אָמַרְתִּי בְחָפְזִי כָּל הָאָדָם כֹּזֵב.

I have loved the Lord - since He hears my voice, my supplications. Since He inclined His ear to me - and in my days, I will call out. The pangs of death have encircled me and the straits of the Pit have found me and I found grief. And in the name of the Lord I called, "Please Lord, Spare my soul." Gracious is the Lord and righteous, and our God acts mercifully. The Lord watches over the silly; I was poor and He has saved me. Return, my soul to your tranquility, since the Lord has favored you. Since You have rescued my soul from death, my eyes from tears, my feet from stumbling. I will walk before the Lord in the lands of the living. I have trusted, when I speak - I am very afflicted. I said in my haste, all men are hypocritical.

What can I give back to the Lord for all that He has favored me? A cup of salvations I will raise up and I will call out in the name of the Lord. My vows to the Lord I will pay, now in front of His entire people. Precious in the eyes of the Lord is the death of His pious ones. Please Lord, since I am Your servant, the son of Your maidservant; You have opened my chains. To You will I offer a thanksgiving offering and I will call out in the name of the Lord. My vows to the Lord I will pay, now in front of His entire people. In the courtyards of the house of the Lord, in your midst, Jerusalem. Halleluyah!

Praise the name of the Lord, all nations; extol Him all peoples. Since His kindness has overwhelmed us and the truth of the Lord is forever. Halleluyah! Thank the Lord, since He is good, since His kindness is forever. Let Israel now say, "Thank the Lord, since He is good, since His kindness is forever." Let the House of Aharon now say, "Thank the Lord, since He is good, since His kindness is forever." Let those that fear the Lord now say, "Thank the Lord, since He is good, since His kindness is forever."

From the strait I have called, Lord; He answered me from the wide space, the Lord. The Lord is for me, I will not fear, what will man do to me? The Lord is for me with my helpers, and I shall glare at those that hate me. It is better to take refuge with the Lord than to trust in man. It is better to take refuge with the Lord than to trust in nobles. All the nations surrounded me - in the name of the Lord, as I will chop them off.

מָה אָשִׁיב לַיי כֹּל תַּגְמוּלוֹהִי עָלָי. כּוֹס יְשׁוּעוֹת אֶשָּׂא וּבְשֵׁם ה' אֶקְרָא. נְדָרַי לַיי אֲשַׁלֵּם נֶגְדָה נָּא לְכָל עַמּוֹ. יָקָר בְּעֵינֵי ה' הַמָּוְתָה לַחֲסִידָיו. אָנָּה ה' כִּי אֲנִי עַבְדֶּךָ, אֲנִי עַבְדְּךָ בֶּן אֲמָתֶךָ, פִּתַּחְתָּ לְמוֹסֵרָי. לְךָ אֶזְבַּח זֶבַח תּוֹדָה וּבְשֵׁם ה' אֶקְרָא. נְדָרַי לַיי אֲשַׁלֵּם נֶגְדָה נָּא לְכָל עַמּוֹ. בְּחַצְרוֹת בֵּית ה', בְּתוֹכֵכִי יְרוּשָׁלַיִם. הַלְלוּיָהּ.

הַלְלוּ אֶת ה' כָּל גּוֹיִם, שַׁבְּחוּהוּ כָּל הָאֻמִּים. כִּי גָבַר עָלֵינוּ חַסְדּוֹ, וֶאֱמֶת ה' לְעוֹלָם. הַלְלוּיָהּ. הוֹדוּ לַיי כִּי טוֹב כִּי לְעוֹלָם חַסְדּוֹ. יֹאמַר נָא יִשְׂרָאֵל כִּי לְעוֹלָם חַסְדּוֹ. יֹאמְרוּ נָא בֵית אַהֲרֹן כִּי לְעוֹלָם חַסְדּוֹ. יֹאמְרוּ נָא יִרְאֵי ה' כִּי לְעוֹלָם חַסְדּוֹ.

מִן הַמֵּצַר קָרָאתִי יָּהּ, עָנָנִי בַמֶּרְחַב יָהּ. ה' לִי, לֹא אִירָא – מַה יַּעֲשֶׂה לִי אָדָם, ה' לִי בְּעֹזְרָי וַאֲנִי אֶרְאֶה בְשֹׂנְאָי. טוֹב לַחֲסוֹת בַּיי מִבְּטֹחַ בָּאָדָם. טוֹב לַחֲסוֹת בַּיי מִבְּטֹחַ בִּנְדִיבִים. כָּל גּוֹיִם סְבָבוּנִי, בְּשֵׁם ה' כִּי אֲמִילַם.

סַבּוּנִי גַם סְבָבוּנִי, בְּשֵׁם ה' כִּי אֲמִילַם. סַבּוּנִי כִדְבֹרִים, דֹּעֲכוּ כְּאֵשׁ קוֹצִים, בְּשֵׁם ה' כִּי אֲמִילַם. דָּחֹה דְחִיתַנִי לִנְפֹּל, וַיי עֲזָרָנִי. עָזִּי וְזִמְרָת יָהּ וַיְהִי לִי לִישׁוּעָה. קוֹל רִנָּה וִישׁוּעָה בְּאָהֳלֵי צַדִּיקִים: יְמִין ה' עֹשָׂה חָיִל, יְמִין ה' רוֹמֵמָה, יְמִין ה' עֹשָׂה חָיִל. לֹא אָמוּת כִּי אֶחְיֶה, וַאֲסַפֵּר מַעֲשֵׂי יָהּ. יַסֹּר יִסְּרַנִּי יָּהּ, וְלַמָּוֶת לֹא נְתָנָנִי. פִּתְחוּ לִי שַׁעֲרֵי צֶדֶק, אָבֹא בָם, אוֹדֶה יָהּ. זֶה הַשַּׁעַר לַיי, צַדִּיקִים יָבֹאוּ בוֹ.

אוֹדְךָ כִּי עֲנִיתָנִי וַתְּהִי לִי לִישׁוּעָה. אוֹדְךָ כִּי עֲנִיתָנִי וַתְּהִי לִי לִישׁוּעָה. אֶבֶן מָאֲסוּ הַבּוֹנִים הָיְתָה לְרֹאשׁ פִּנָּה. אֶבֶן מָאֲסוּ הַבּוֹנִים הָיְתָה לְרֹאשׁ פִּנָּה. מֵאֵת ה' הָיְתָה זֹּאת הִיא נִפְלָאת בְּעֵינֵינוּ. מֵאֵת ה' הָיְתָה זֹּאת הִיא נִפְלָאת בְּעֵינֵינוּ. זֶה הַיּוֹם עָשָׂה ה'. נָגִילָה וְנִשְׂמְחָה בוֹ. זֶה הַיּוֹם עָשָׂה ה'. נָגִילָה וְנִשְׂמְחָה בוֹ.

אָנָּא ה', הוֹשִׁיעָה נָּא. אָנָּא ה', הוֹשִׁיעָה נָּא. אָנָּא ה', הַצְלִיחָה נָא. אָנָּא ה', הַצְלִיחָה נָא.

They surrounded me, they also encircled me - in the name of the Lord, as I will chop them off. They surrounded me like bees, they were extinguished like a fire of thorns - in the name of the Lord, as I will chop them off. You have surely pushed me to fall, but the Lord helped me. My boldness and song is the Lord, and He has become my salvation. The sound of happy song and salvation is in the tents of the righteous, the right hand of the Lord acts powerfully. I will not die but rather I will live and tell over the acts of the Lord. The Lord has surely chastised me, but He has not given me over to death. Open up for me the gates of righteousness; I will enter them, thank the Lord. This is the gate of the Lord, the righteous will enter it.

I will thank You, since You answered me and You have become my salvation. The stone that was left by the builders has become the main cornerstone. From the Lord was this, it is wondrous in our eyes. This is the day of the Lord, let us exult and rejoice upon it.

Please, Lord, save us now; please, Lord, give us success now!

Blessed be the one who comes in the name of the Lord, we have blessed you from the house of the Lord. God is the Lord, and He has illuminated us; tie up the festival offering with ropes until it reaches the corners of the altar. You are my Power and I will Thank You; my God and I will exalt You. Thank the Lord, since He is good, since His kindness is forever.

All of your works shall praise You, Lord our God, and your pious ones, the righteous ones who do Your will; and all of Your people, the House of Israel will thank and bless in joyful song: and extol and glorify, and exalt and acclaim, and sanctify and coronate Your name, our King. Since, You it is good to thank, and to Your name it is pleasant to sing, since from always and forever are you the Power.

בָּרוּךְ הַבָּא בְּשֵׁם ה׳, בֵּרַכְנוּכֶם מִבֵּית ה׳. בָּרוּךְ הַבָּא בְּשֵׁם ה׳, בֵּרַכְנוּכֶם מִבֵּית ה׳. אֵל ה׳ וַיָּאֶר לָנוּ. אִסְרוּ חַג בַּעֲבֹתִים עַד קַרְנוֹת הַמִּזְבֵּחַ. אֵל ה׳ וַיָּאֶר לָנוּ. אִסְרוּ חַג בַּעֲבֹתִים עַד קַרְנוֹת הַמִּזְבֵּחַ. אֵלִי אַתָּה וְאוֹדֶךָּ, אֱלֹהַי – אֲרוֹמְמֶךָּ. אֵלִי אַתָּה וְאוֹדֶךָּ, אֱלֹהַי – אֲרוֹמְמֶךָּ. הוֹדוּ לַיי כִּי טוֹב, כִּי לְעוֹלָם חַסְדּוֹ. הוֹדוּ לַיי כִּי טוֹב, כִּי לְעוֹלָם חַסְדּוֹ.

יְהַלְלוּךָ ה׳ אֱלֹהֵינוּ כָּל מַעֲשֶׂיךָ, וַחֲסִידֶיךָ צַדִּיקִים עוֹשֵׂי רְצוֹנֶךָ, וְכָל עַמְּךָ בֵּית יִשְׂרָאֵל בְּרִנָּה יוֹדוּ וִיבָרְכוּ, וִישַׁבְּחוּ וִיפָאֲרוּ, וִירוֹמְמוּ וְיַעֲרִיצוּ, וְיַקְדִּישׁוּ וְיַמְלִיכוּ אֶת שִׁמְךָ, מַלְכֵּנוּ. כִּי לְךָ טוֹב לְהוֹדוֹת וּלְשִׁמְךָ נָאֶה לְזַמֵּר, כִּי מֵעוֹלָם וְעַד עוֹלָם אַתָּה אֵל.

Give thanks to the Lord!

OH. MY. GOD.

Songs of Praise and Thanks

Thank the Lord, since He is good, since His kindness is forever. Thank the Power of powers since His kindness is forever. To the Master of masters, since His kindness is forever. To the One who alone does wondrously great deeds, since His kindness is forever. To the one who made the Heavens with discernment, since His kindness is forever. To the One who spread the earth over the waters, since His kindness is forever. To the One who made great lights, since His kindness is forever. The sun to rule in the day, since His kindness is forever. The moon and the stars to rule in the night, since His kindness is forever. To the One that smote Egypt through their firstborn, since His kindness is forever. And He took Israel out from among them, since His kindness is forever. With a strong hand and an outstretched forearm, since His kindness is forever. To the One who cut up the Reed Sea into strips, since His kindness is forever. And He made Israel to pass through it, since His kindness is forever. And He jolted Pharaoh and his troop in the Reed Sea, since His kindness is forever. To the One who led his people in the wilderness, since His kindness is forever. To the One who smote great kings, since His kindness is forever. And he killed mighty kings, since His kindness is forever.

מזמורי הודיה

הוֹדוּ לַיי כִּי טוֹב כִּי לְעוֹלָם חַסְדּוֹ. הוֹדוּ לֵאלֹהֵי הָאֱלֹהִים כִּי לְעוֹלָם חַסְדּוֹ. הוֹדוּ לַאֲדֹנֵי הָאֲדֹנִים כִּי לְעוֹלָם חַסְדּוֹ. לְעֹשֵׂה נִפְלָאוֹת גְּדֹלוֹת לְבַדּוֹ כִּי לְעוֹלָם חַסְדּוֹ. לְעֹשֵׂה הַשָּׁמַיִם בִּתְבוּנָה כִּי לְעוֹלָם חַסְדּוֹ. לְרוֹקַע הָאָרֶץ עַל הַמָּיִם כִּי לְעוֹלָם חַסְדּוֹ. לְעֹשֵׂה אוֹרִים גְּדֹלִים כִּי לְעוֹלָם חַסְדּוֹ. אֶת הַשֶּׁמֶשׁ לְמֶמְשֶׁלֶת בַּיּוֹם כִּי לְעוֹלָם חַסְדּוֹ. אֶת הַיָּרֵחַ וְכוֹכָבִים לְמֶמְשְׁלוֹת בַּלַּיְלָה כִּי לְעוֹלָם חַסְדּוֹ. לְמַכֵּה מִצְרַיִם בִּבְכוֹרֵיהֶם כִּי לְעוֹלָם חַסְדּוֹ. וַיּוֹצֵא יִשְׂרָאֵל מִתּוֹכָם כִּי לְעוֹלָם חַסְדּוֹ. בְּיָד חֲזָקָה וּבִזְרוֹעַ נְטוּיָה כִּי לְעוֹלָם חַסְדּוֹ. לְגֹזֵר יַם סוּף לִגְזָרִים כִּי לְעוֹלָם חַסְדּוֹ. וְהֶעֱבִיר יִשְׂרָאֵל בְּתוֹכוֹ כִּי לְעוֹלָם חַסְדּוֹ. וְנִעֵר פַּרְעֹה וְחֵילוֹ בְיַם סוּף כִּי לְעוֹלָם חַסְדּוֹ. לְמוֹלִיךְ עַמּוֹ בַּמִּדְבָּר כִּי לְעוֹלָם חַסְדּוֹ. לְמַכֵּה מְלָכִים גְּדֹלִים כִּי לְעוֹלָם חַסְדּוֹ. וַיַּהֲרֹג מְלָכִים אַדִּירִים כִּי לְעוֹלָם חַסְדּוֹ.

Sichon, king of the Amorite, since His kindness is forever. And Og, king of the Bashan, since His kindness is forever. And he gave their land as an inheritance, since His kindness is forever. An inheritance for Israel, His servant, since His kindness is forever. That in our lowliness, He remembered us, since His kindness is forever. And he delivered us from our adversaries, since His kindness is forever. He gives bread to all flesh, since His kindness is forever. Thank the Power of the heavens, since His kindness is forever.

The soul of every living being shall bless Your Name, Lord our God; the spirit of all flesh shall glorify and exalt Your remembrance always, our King. From the world and until the world, You are the Power, and other than You we have no king, redeemer, or savior, restorer, rescuer, provider, and merciful one in every time of distress and anguish; we have no king, besides You! God of the first ones and the last ones, God of all creatures, Master of all Generations, Who is praised through a multitude of praises, Who guides His world with kindness and His creatures with mercy. The Lord neither slumbers nor sleeps. He who rouses the sleepers and awakens the dozers; He who makes the mute speak, and frees the captives, and supports the falling, and straightens the bent. We thank You alone.

לְסִיחוֹן מֶלֶךְ הָאֱמֹרִי כִּי לְעוֹלָם חַסְדּוֹ. וּלְעוֹג מֶלֶךְ הַבָּשָׁן כִּי לְעוֹלָם חַסְדּוֹ. וְנָתַן אַרְצָם לְנַחֲלָה כִּי לְעוֹלָם חַסְדּוֹ. נַחֲלָה לְיִשְׂרָאֵל עַבְדּוֹ כִּי לְעוֹלָם חַסְדּוֹ. שֶׁבְּשִׁפְלֵנוּ זָכַר לָנוּ כִּי לְעוֹלָם חַסְדּוֹ. וַיִּפְרְקֵנוּ מִצָּרֵינוּ כִּי לְעוֹלָם חַסְדּוֹ. נֹתֵן לֶחֶם לְכָל בָּשָׂר כִּי לְעוֹלָם חַסְדּוֹ. הוֹדוּ לְאֵל הַשָּׁמַיִם כִּי לְעוֹלָם חַסְדּוֹ.

נִשְׁמַת כָּל חַי תְּבָרֵךְ אֶת שִׁמְךָ, ה' אֱלֹהֵינוּ, וְרוּחַ כָּל בָּשָׂר תְּפָאֵר וּתְרוֹמֵם זִכְרְךָ, מַלְכֵּנוּ, תָּמִיד. מִן הָעוֹלָם וְעַד הָעוֹלָם אַתָּה אֵל, וּמִבַּלְעָדֶיךָ אֵין לָנוּ מֶלֶךְ גּוֹאֵל וּמוֹשִׁיעַ, פּוֹדֶה וּמַצִּיל וּמְפַרְנֵס וּמְרַחֵם בְּכָל עֵת צָרָה וְצוּקָה. אֵין לָנוּ מֶלֶךְ אֶלָּא אָתָּה. אֱלֹהֵי הָרִאשׁוֹנִים וְהָאַחֲרוֹנִים, אֱלוֹהַּ כָּל בְּרִיּוֹת, אֲדוֹן כָּל תּוֹלָדוֹת, הַמְהֻלָּל בְּרֹב הַתִּשְׁבָּחוֹת, הַמְנַהֵג עוֹלָמוֹ בְּחֶסֶד וּבְרִיּוֹתָיו בְּרַחֲמִים. וַיי לֹא יָנוּם וְלֹא יִישָׁן – הַמְעוֹרֵר יְשֵׁנִים וְהַמֵּקִיץ נִרְדָּמִים, וְהַמֵּשִׂיחַ אִלְּמִים וְהַמַּתִּיר אֲסוּרִים וְהַסּוֹמֵךְ נוֹפְלִים וְהַזּוֹקֵף כְּפוּפִים. לְךָ לְבַדְּךָ אֲנַחְנוּ מוֹדִים.

אִלּוּ פִינוּ מָלֵא שִׁירָה כַּיָּם, וּלְשׁוֹנֵנוּ רִנָּה כַּהֲמוֹן גַּלָּיו, וְשִׂפְתוֹתֵינוּ שֶׁבַח כְּמֶרְחֲבֵי רָקִיעַ, וְעֵינֵינוּ מְאִירוֹת כַּשֶּׁמֶשׁ וְכַיָּרֵחַ, וְיָדֵינוּ פְרוּשׂוֹת כְּנִשְׁרֵי שָׁמַיִם, וְרַגְלֵינוּ קַלּוֹת כָּאַיָּלוֹת – אֵין אֲנַחְנוּ מַסְפִּיקִים לְהוֹדוֹת לְךָ, ה' אֱלֹהֵינוּ וֵאלֹהֵי אֲבוֹתֵינוּ, וּלְבָרֵךְ אֶת שְׁמֶךָ עַל אַחַת מֵאֶלֶף, אַלְפֵי אֲלָפִים וְרִבֵּי רְבָבוֹת פְּעָמִים הַטּוֹבוֹת שֶׁעָשִׂיתָ עִם אֲבוֹתֵינוּ וְעִמָּנוּ. מִמִּצְרַיִם גְּאַלְתָּנוּ, ה' אֱלֹהֵינוּ, וּמִבֵּית עֲבָדִים פְּדִיתָנוּ, בְּרָעָב זַנְתָּנוּ וּבְשָׂבָע כִּלְכַּלְתָּנוּ, מֵחֶרֶב הִצַּלְתָּנוּ וּמִדֶּבֶר מִלַּטְתָּנוּ, וּמֵחֳלָיִם רָעִים וְנֶאֱמָנִים דִּלִּיתָנוּ.

עַד הֵנָּה עֲזָרוּנוּ רַחֲמֶיךָ וְלֹא עֲזָבוּנוּ חֲסָדֶיךָ, וְאַל תִּטְּשֵׁנוּ, ה' אֱלֹהֵינוּ, לָנֶצַח. עַל כֵּן אֵבָרִים שֶׁפִּלַּגְתָּ בָּנוּ וְרוּחַ וּנְשָׁמָה שֶׁנָּפַחְתָּ בְּאַפֵּינוּ וְלָשׁוֹן אֲשֶׁר שַׂמְתָּ בְּפִינוּ – הֵן הֵם יוֹדוּ וִיבָרְכוּ וִישַׁבְּחוּ וִיפָאֲרוּ וִירוֹמְמוּ וְיַעֲרִיצוּ וְיַקְדִּישׁוּ וְיַמְלִיכוּ אֶת שִׁמְךָ מַלְכֵּנוּ.

Were our mouth as full of song as the sea, and our tongue as full of joyous song as its multitude of waves, and our lips as full of praise as the breadth of the heavens, and our eyes as sparkling as the sun and the moon, and our hands as outspread as the eagles of the sky and our feet as swift as deers - we still could not thank You sufficiently, Lord our God and God of our ancestors, and to bless Your Name for one thousandth of the thousand of thousands of thousands, and myriad myriads, of goodnesses that You performed for our ancestors and for us. From Egypt, Lord our God, did you redeem us and from the house of slaves you restored us. In famine You nourished us, and in plenty you sustained us. From the sword you saved us, and from plague you spared us; and from severe and enduring diseases you delivered us.

Until now Your mercy has helped us, and Your kindness has not forsaken us; and do not abandon us, Lord our God, forever. Therefore, the limbs that You set within us and the spirit and soul that You breathed into our nostrils, and the tongue that You placed in our mouth - verily, they shall thank and bless and praise and glorify, and exalt and revere, and sanctify and coronate Your name, our King.

כִּי כָל פֶּה לְךָ יוֹדֶה, וְכָל לָשׁוֹן לְךָ תִשָּׁבַע, וְכָל בֶּרֶךְ לְךָ תִכְרַע, וְכָל קוֹמָה לְפָנֶיךָ תִשְׁתַּחֲוֶה, וְכָל לְבָבוֹת יִירָאוּךָ, וְכָל קֶרֶב וּכְלָיוֹת יְזַמְּרוּ לִשְׁמֶךָ. כַּדָּבָר שֶׁכָּתוּב, כָּל עַצְמֹתַי תֹּאמַרְנָה, ה' מִי כָמוֹךָ מַצִּיל עָנִי מֵחָזָק מִמֶּנּוּ וְעָנִי וְאֶבְיוֹן מִגֹּזְלוֹ. מִי יִדְמֶה לָּךְ וּמִי יִשְׁוֶה לָּךְ וּמִי יַעֲרָךְ לָךְ הָאֵל הַגָּדוֹל, הַגִּבּוֹר וְהַנּוֹרָא, אֵל עֶלְיוֹן, קֹנֵה שָׁמַיִם וָאָרֶץ. נְהַלֶּלְךָ וּנְשַׁבֵּחֲךָ וּנְפָאֶרְךָ וּנְבָרֵךְ אֶת שֵׁם קָדְשֶׁךָ, כָּאָמוּר: לְדָוִד, בָּרְכִי נַפְשִׁי אֶת ה' וְכָל קְרָבַי אֶת שֵׁם קָדְשׁוֹ. הָאֵל בְּתַעֲצֻמוֹת עֻזֶּךָ, הַגָּדוֹל בִּכְבוֹד שְׁמֶךָ, הַגִּבּוֹר לָנֶצַח וְהַנּוֹרָא בְּנוֹרְאוֹתֶיךָ, הַמֶּלֶךְ הַיּוֹשֵׁב עַל כִּסֵּא רָם וְנִשָּׂא. שׁוֹכֵן עַד מָרוֹם וְקָדוֹשׁ שְׁמוֹ. וְכָתוּב: רַנְּנוּ צַדִּיקִים בַּיָי, לַיְשָׁרִים נָאוָה תְהִלָּה. בְּפִי יְשָׁרִים תִּתְהַלָּל, וּבְדִבְרֵי צַדִּיקִים תִּתְבָּרַךְ, וּבִלְשׁוֹן חֲסִידִים תִּתְרוֹמָם, וּבְקֶרֶב קְדוֹשִׁים תִּתְקַדָּשׁ.

For every mouth shall offer thanks to You; and every tongue shall swear allegiance to You; and every knee shall bend to You; and every upright one shall prostrate himself before You; all hearts shall fear You; and all innermost feelings and thoughts shall sing praises to Your name, as the matter is written, "All my bones shall say, 'Lord, who is like You? You save the poor man from one who is stronger than he, the poor and destitute from the one who would rob him.'" Who is similar to You and who is equal to You and who can be compared to You, O great, strong and awesome Power, O highest Power, Creator of the heavens and the earth. We shall praise and extol and glorify and bless Your holy name, as it is stated, " [A Psalm] of David. Bless the Lord, O my soul; and all that is within me, His holy name." The Power, in Your powerful boldness; the Great, in the glory of Your name; the Strong One forever; the King who sits on His high and elevated throne. He who dwells always; lofty and holy is His name. And as it is written, "Sing joyfully to the Lord, righteous ones, praise is beautiful from the upright." By the mouth of the upright You shall be praised; By the lips of the righteous shall You be blessed; By the tongue of the devout shall You be exalted; And among the holy shall You be sanctified.

And in the assemblies of the myriads of Your people, the House of Israel, in joyous song will Your name be glorified, our King, in each and every generation; as it is the duty of all creatures, before You, Lord our God, and God of our ancestors, to thank, to praise, to extol, to glorify, to exalt, to lavish, to bless, to raise high and to acclaim - beyond the words of the songs and praises of David, the son of Yishai, Your servant, Your anointed one.

May Your name be praised forever, our King, the Power, the Great and holy King - in the heavens and in the earth. Since for You it is pleasant - O Lord our God and God of our ancestors - song and lauding, praise and hymn, boldness and dominion, triumph, greatness and strength, psalm and splendor, holiness and kingship, blessings and thanksgivings, from now and forever. Blessed are You Lord, Power, King exalted through laudings, Power of thanksgivings, Master of Wonders, who chooses the songs of hymn - King, Power of the life of the worlds.

Fourth Cup of Wine

Blessed are You, Lord our God, King of the universe, who creates the fruit of the vine.

וּבְמַקְהֲלוֹת רִבְבוֹת עַמְּךָ בֵּית יִשְׂרָאֵל בְּרִנָּה יִתְפָּאֵר שִׁמְךָ, מַלְכֵּנוּ, בְּכָל דּוֹר וָדוֹר, שֶׁכֵּן חוֹבַת כָּל הַיְצוּרִים לְפָנֶיךָ, ה' אֱלֹהֵינוּ וֵאלֹהֵי אֲבוֹתֵינוּ, לְהוֹדוֹת לְהַלֵּל לְשַׁבֵּחַ, לְפָאֵר לְרוֹמֵם לְהַדֵּר לְבָרֵךְ, לְעַלֵּה וּלְקַלֵּס עַל כָּל דִּבְרֵי שִׁירוֹת וְתִשְׁבָּחוֹת דָּוִד בֶּן יִשַׁי עַבְדְּךָ מְשִׁיחֶךָ.

יִשְׁתַּבַּח שִׁמְךָ לָעַד מַלְכֵּנוּ, הָאֵל הַמֶּלֶךְ הַגָּדוֹל וְהַקָּדוֹשׁ בַּשָּׁמַיִם וּבָאָרֶץ, כִּי לְךָ נָאֶה, ה' אֱלֹהֵינוּ וֵאלֹהֵי אֲבוֹתֵינוּ, שִׁיר וּשְׁבָחָה, הַלֵּל וְזִמְרָה, עֹז וּמֶמְשָׁלָה, נֶצַח, גְּדֻלָּה וּגְבוּרָה, תְּהִלָּה וְתִפְאֶרֶת, קְדֻשָּׁה וּמַלְכוּת, בְּרָכוֹת וְהוֹדָאוֹת מֵעַתָּה וְעַד עוֹלָם. בָּרוּךְ אַתָּה ה', אֵל מֶלֶךְ גָּדוֹל בַּתִּשְׁבָּחוֹת, אֵל הַהוֹדָאוֹת, אֲדוֹן הַנִּפְלָאוֹת, הַבּוֹחֵר בְּשִׁירֵי זִמְרָה, מֶלֶךְ אֵל חֵי הָעוֹלָמִים.

כוס רביעית

בָּרוּךְ אַתָּה ה', אֱלֹהֵינוּ מֶלֶךְ הָעוֹלָם בּוֹרֵא פְּרִי הַגָּפֶן.

We drink while reclining to the left.

Blessed are You, Lord our God, King of the universe, for the vine and for the fruit of the vine; and for the bounty of the field; and for a desirable, good and broad land, which You wanted to give to our fathers, to eat from its fruit and to be satiated from its goodness. Please have mercy, Lord our God upon Israel Your people; and upon Jerusalem, Your city: and upon Zion, the dwelling place of Your glory; and upon Your altar; and upon Your sanctuary; and build Jerusalem Your holy city quickly in our days, and bring us up into it and gladden us in its building; and we shall eat from its fruit, and be satiated from its goodness, and bless You in holiness and purity. [On Shabbat: And may you be pleased to embolden us on this Shabbat day] and gladden us on this day of the Festival of Matzot. Since You, Lord, are good and do good to all, we thank You for the land and for the fruit of the vine.

Blessed are You, Lord, for the land and for the fruit of the vine

וְשׁוֹתֶה בַּהֲסִיבַת שְׂמֹאל.

בָּרוּךְ אַתָּה ה' אֱלֹהֵינוּ מֶלֶךְ הָעוֹלָם, עַל הַגֶּפֶן וְעַל פְּרִי הַגֶּפֶן, עַל תְּנוּבַת הַשָּׂדֶה וְעַל אֶרֶץ חֶמְדָּה טוֹבָה וּרְחָבָה שֶׁרָצִיתָ וְהִנְחַלְתָּ לַאֲבוֹתֵינוּ לֶאֱכֹל מִפִּרְיָהּ וְלִשְׂבֹּעַ מִטּוּבָהּ. רַחֵם נָא ה' אֱלֹהֵינוּ עַל יִשְׂרָאֵל עַמֶּךָ וְעַל יְרוּשָׁלַיִם עִירֶךָ וְעַל צִיּוֹן מִשְׁכַּן כְּבוֹדֶךָ וְעַל מִזְבְּחֶךָ וְעַל הֵיכָלֶךָ וּבְנֵה יְרוּשָׁלַיִם עִיר הַקֹּדֶשׁ בִּמְהֵרָה בְיָמֵינוּ וְהַעֲלֵנוּ לְתוֹכָהּ וְשַׂמְּחֵנוּ בְּבִנְיָנָהּ וְנֹאכַל מִפִּרְיָהּ וְנִשְׂבַּע מִטּוּבָהּ וּנְבָרֶכְךָ עָלֶיהָ בִּקְדֻשָּׁה וּבְטָהֳרָה [בשבת: וּרְצֵה וְהַחֲלִיצֵנוּ בְּיוֹם הַשַּׁבָּת הַזֶּה] וְשַׂמְּחֵנוּ בְּיוֹם חַג הַמַּצּוֹת הַזֶּה, כִּי אַתָּה ה' טוֹב וּמֵטִיב לַכֹּל, וְנוֹדֶה לְךָ עַל הָאָרֶץ וְעַל פְּרִי הַגָּפֶן.

בָּרוּךְ אַתָּה ה', עַל הָאָרֶץ וְעַל פְּרִי הַגָּפֶן.

S2E10: The One with Russ
Rachel: We went through a LOT of wine tonight, you guys.
Monica: Really? I only had two glasses.
Joey: I just had a glass.
Phoebe: Two.
Rachel: I had one glass.
Chandler: I had about a mug full…
Rachel: Ok, so that's, that's what about two bottles…
Monica: So what? So we drank a lot tonight.

NIRTZAH

Accepted

Completed is the Seder of Pesach according to Its law, according to all its judgement and statute. Just as we have merited to arrange it, so too, may we merit to do [its sacrifice]. Pure One who dwells in the habitation, raise up the congregation of the community, which whom can count. Bring close, lead the plantings of the sapling, redeemed, to Zion in joy.

Next year, let us be in Jerusalem!

On the first night we say:
And so, it was in the middle of the night.

Then, most of the miracles did You wondrously do at night, at the first of the watches this night.

נרצה

חֲסַל סִדּוּר פֶּסַח כְּהִלְכָתוֹ, כְּכָל מִשְׁפָּטוֹ וְחֻקָּתוֹ. כַּאֲשֶׁר זָכִינוּ לְסַדֵּר אוֹתוֹ כֵּן נִזְכֶּה לַעֲשׂוֹתוֹ. זָךְ שׁוֹכֵן מְעוֹנָה, קוֹמֵם קְהַל עֲדַת מִי מָנָה. בְּקָרוֹב נַהֵל נִטְעֵי כַנָּה פְּדוּיִם לְצִיּוֹן בְּרִנָּה.

לְשָׁנָה הַבָּאָה בִּירוּשָׁלַיִם הַבְּנוּיָה.

בליל ראשון אומרים:
וּבְכֵן וַיְהִי בַּחֲצִי הַלַּיְלָה.

אָז רוֹב נִסִּים הִפְלֵאתָ בַּלַּיְלָה, בְּרֹאשׁ אַשְׁמוֹרֶת זֶה הַלַּיְלָה.

גֵּר צֶדֶק נִצַּחְתּוֹ כְּנֶחֱלַק לוֹ לַיְלָה,
וַיְהִי בַּחֲצִי הַלַּיְלָה.

דַּנְתָּ מֶלֶךְ גְּרָר בַּחֲלוֹם הַלַּיְלָה,
הִפְחַדְתָּ אֲרַמִּי בְּאֶמֶשׁ לַיְלָה.

וַיָּשַׂר יִשְׂרָאֵל לְמַלְאָךְ וַיּוּכַל לוֹ
לַיְלָה, וַיְהִי בַּחֲצִי הַלַּיְלָה.

זֶרַע בְּכוֹרֵי פַתְרוֹס מָחַצְתָּ בַּחֲצִי
הַלַּיְלָה, חֵילָם לֹא מָצְאוּ בְקוּמָם
בַּלַּיְלָה, טִיסַת נְגִיד חֲרֹשֶׁת
סִלִּיתָ בְּכוֹכְבֵי לַיְלָה, וַיְהִי בַּחֲצִי
הַלַּיְלָה.

יָעַץ מְחָרֵף לְנוֹפֵף אִוּוּי, הוֹבַשְׁתָּ
פְגָרָיו בַּלַּיְלָה, כָּרַע בֵּל וּמַצָּבוֹ
בְּאִישׁוֹן לַיְלָה, לְאִישׁ חֲמוּדוֹת
נִגְלָה רָז חֲזוֹת לַיְלָה, וַיְהִי בַּחֲצִי
הַלַּיְלָה.

מִשְׁתַּכֵּר בִּכְלֵי קֹדֶשׁ נֶהֱרַג בּוֹ
בַּלַּיְלָה, נוֹשַׁע מִבּוֹר אֲרָיוֹת
פּוֹתֵר בְּעִתּוּתֵי לַיְלָה, שִׂנְאָה
נָטַר אֲגָגִי וְכָתַב סְפָרִים בַּלַּיְלָה,
וַיְהִי בַּחֲצִי הַלַּיְלָה.

A righteous convert did you make victorious when it was divided for him at night [referring to Avraham in his war against the four kings], and it was in the middle of the night.

You judged the king of Gerrar [Avimelekh] in a dream of the night; you frightened an Aramean [Lavan] in the dark of the night;

and Yisrael dominated an angel and was able to withstand Him at night, and it was in the middle of the night.

You crushed the firstborn of Patros [Pharaoh] in the middle of the night, their wealth they did not find when they got up at night; the attack of the leader Charoshet [Sisera] did you sweep away by the stars of the night, and it was in the middle of the night.

The blasphemer [Sancheriv whose servants blasphemed when trying to discourage the inhabitants of Jerusalem] counseled to wave off the desired ones, You made him wear his corpses on his head at night; Bel and his pedestal were bent in the pitch of night [in Nevuchadnezar's dream]; to the man of delight [Daniel] was revealed the secret visions at night, and it was in the middle of the night.

The one who got drunk [Balshatsar] from the holy vessels was killed on that night, the one saved from the pit of lions [Daniel] interpreted the scary visions of the night; hatred was preserved by the Agagite [Haman] and he wrote books at night, and it was in the middle of the night.

עוֹרַרְתָּ נִצְחֲךָ עָלָיו בְּנֶדֶד שְׁנַת לַיְלָה. פּוּרָה תִדְרוֹךְ לְשׁוֹמֵר מַה מִלַּיְלָה, צָרַח כַּשּׁוֹמֵר וְשָׂח אָתָא בֹקֶר וְגַם לַיְלָה, וַיְהִי בַּחֲצִי הַלַּיְלָה.

קָרֵב יוֹם אֲשֶׁר הוּא לֹא יוֹם וְלֹא לַיְלָה, רָם הוֹדַע כִּי לְךָ הַיּוֹם אַף לְךָ הַלַּיְלָה, שׁוֹמְרִים הַפְקֵד לְעִירְךָ כָּל הַיּוֹם וְכָל הַלַּיְלָה, תָּאִיר כְּאוֹר יוֹם חֶשְׁכַּת לַיְלָה, וַיְהִי בַּחֲצִי הַלַּיְלָה.

You aroused your victory upon him by disturbing the sleep of night [of Achashverosh], You will stomp the wine press for the one who guards from anything at night; He yelled like a guard and spoke, "the morning has come and also the night," and it was in the middle of the night.

Bring close the day which is not day and not night [referring to the end of days, High One, make known that Yours is the day and also Yours is the night, guards appoint for Your city all the day and all the night, illuminate like the light of the day, the darkness of the night, and it was in the middle of the night.

Zevach Pesach // זבח פסח

On the second night, outside of Israel: And so "And you shall say, 'it is the Pesach sacrifice'".

בְּלֵיל שֵׁנִי בחו"ל: וּבְכֵן וַאֲמַרְתֶּם זֶבַח פֶּסַח.

The boldness of Your strong deeds did you wondrously show at Pesach; at the head of all the holidays did You raise Pesach; You revealed to the Ezrachite [Avraham], midnight of the night of Pesach. "And you shall say, 'it is the Pesach sacrifice.'"

אֹמֶץ גְּבוּרוֹתֶיךָ הִפְלֵאתָ בַּפֶּסַח, בְּרֹאשׁ כָּל מוֹעֲדוֹת נִשֵּׂאתָ פֶּסַח. גִּלִּיתָ לְאֶזְרָחִי חֲצוֹת לֵיל פֶּסַח, וַאֲמַרְתֶּם זֶבַח פֶּסַח.

Upon his doors did You knock at the heat of the day on Pesach; he sustained shining ones [angels] with cakes of matzah on Pesach; and to the cattle he ran, in commemoration of the bull that was set up for Pesach. "And you shall say, 'it is the Pesach sacrifice.'"

דְּלָתָיו דָּפַקְתָּ כְּחֹם הַיּוֹם בַּפֶּסַח, הִסְעִיד נוֹצְצִים עֻגוֹת מַצּוֹת בַּפֶּסַח, וְאֶל הַבָּקָר רָץ זֵכֶר לְשׁוֹר עֵרֶךְ פֶּסַח, וַאֲמַרְתֶּם זֶבַח פֶּסַח.

The Sodomites caused Him indignation and He set them on fire on Pesach; Lot was rescued from them and matzot did he bake at the end of Pesach; He swept the land of Mof and Nof on Pesach. "And you shall say, 'it is the Pesach sacrifice.'"

זוֹעֲמוּ סְדוֹמִים וְלֹהֲטוּ בָּאֵשׁ בַּפֶּסַח, חֻלַּץ לוֹט מֵהֶם וּמַצּוֹת אָפָה בְּקֵץ פֶּסַח, טִאטֵאתָ אַדְמַת מוֹף וְנוֹף בְּעָבְרְךָ בַּפֶּסַח. וַאֲמַרְתֶּם זֶבַח פֶּסַח.

The head of every firstborn did You crush on the guarded night of Pesach; Powerful One, over the firstborn son did You pass over with the blood on Pesach; so as to not let the destroyer come into my gates on Pesach. "And you shall say, 'it is the Pesach sacrifice.'"

יָהּ רֹאשׁ כָּל הוֹן מָחַצְתָּ בְּלֵיל שִׁמּוּר פֶּסַח, כַּבִּיר, עַל בֵּן בְּכוֹר פָּסַחְתָּ בְּדַם פֶּסַח, לְבִלְתִּי תֵּת מַשְׁחִית לָבֹא בִּפְתָחַי בַּפֶּסַח, וַאֲמַרְתֶּם זֶבַח פֶּסַח.

מְסֻגֶּרֶת סֻגְּרָה בְּעִתּוֹתֵי פֶּסַח, נִשְׁמְדָה מִדְיָן בִּצְלִיל שְׂעוֹרֵי עֹמֶר פֶּסַח, שׂוֹרְפוּ מִשְׁמַנֵּי פּוּל וְלוּד בִּיקַד יְקוֹד פֶּסַח, וַאֲמַרְתֶּם זֶבַח פֶּסַח.

עוֹד הַיּוֹם בְּנֹב לַעֲמוֹד עַד גָּעָה עוֹנַת פֶּסַח, פַּס יָד כָּתְבָה לְקַעֲקֵעַ צוּל בַּפֶּסַח, צָפֹה הַצָּפִית עָרוֹךְ הַשֻּׁלְחָן בַּפֶּסַח, וַאֲמַרְתֶּם זֶבַח פֶּסַח.

קָהָל כִּנְּסָה הֲדַסָּה לְשַׁלֵּשׁ צוֹם בַּפֶּסַח, רֹאשׁ מִבֵּית רָשָׁע מָחַצְתָּ בְּעֵץ חֲמִשִּׁים בַּפֶּסַח, שְׁתֵּי אֵלֶּה רֶגַע תָּבִיא לְעוּצִית בַּפֶּסַח, תָּעֹז יָדְךָ תָּרוּם יְמִינְךָ כְּלֵיל הִתְקַדֵּשׁ חַג פֶּסַח, וַאֲמַרְתֶּם זֶבַח פֶּסַח.

כִּי לוֹ נָאֶה, כִּי לוֹ יָאֶה.

אַדִּיר בִּמְלוּכָה, בָּחוּר כַּהֲלָכָה, גְּדוּדָיו יֹאמְרוּ לוֹ: לְךָ וּלְךָ, לְךָ כִּי לְךָ, לְךָ אַף לְךָ, לְךָ ה' הַמַּמְלָכָה, כִּי לוֹ נָאֶה, כִּי לוֹ יָאֶה.

דָּגוּל בִּמְלוּכָה, הָדוּר כַּהֲלָכָה, וְתִיקָיו יֹאמְרוּ לוֹ: לְךָ וּלְךָ, לְךָ כִּי לְךָ, לְךָ אַף לְךָ, לְךָ ה' הַמַּמְלָכָה, כִּי לוֹ נָאֶה, כִּי לוֹ יָאֶה.

The enclosed one [Jericho] was enclosed in the season of Pesach; Midian was destroyed with a portion of the omer-barley on Pesach; from the fat of Pul and Lud was burnt in pyres on Pesach. "And you shall say, 'it is the Pesach sacrifice'"

Still today [Sancheriv will go no further than] to stand in Nov, until he cried at the time of Pesach; a palm of the hand wrote to rip up the deep one [the Bayblonian one - Balshatsar] on Pesach; set up the watch, set the table [referring to Balshatsar] on Pesach. "And you shall say, 'it is the Pesach sacrifice'"

The congregation did Hadassah [Esther] bring in to triple a fast on Pesach; the head of the house of evil [Haman] did you crush on a tree of fifty [amot] on Pesach; these two [plagues as per] will you bring in an instant to the Utsi [Esav] on Pesach; embolden Your hand, raise Your right hand, as on the night You were sanctified on the festival of Pesach. "And you shall say, 'it is the Pesach sacrifice'"

Since for Him it is pleasant, for Him it is suited.

Mighty in rulership, properly chosen, his troops shall say to Him, "Yours and Yours, Yours since it is Yours, Yours and even Yours, Yours, Lord is the kingdom; since for Him it is pleasant, for Him it is suited."

Noted in rulership, properly splendid, His distinguished ones will say to him, "Yours and Yours, Yours since it is Yours, Yours and even Yours, Yours, Lord is the kingdom; since for Him it is pleasant, for Him it is suited."

Meritorious in rulership, properly robust, His scribes shall say to him, "Yours and Yours, Yours since it is Yours, Yours and even Yours, Yours, Lord is the kingdom; since for Him it is pleasant, for Him it is suited."	זַכַּאי בִּמְלוּכָה, חָסִין כַּהֲלָכָה טַפְסְרָיו יֹאמְרוּ לוֹ: לְךָ וּלְךָ, לְךָ כִּי לְךָ, לְךָ אַף לְךָ, לְךָ ה' הַמַּמְלָכָה, כִּי לוֹ נָאֶה, כִּי לוֹ יָאֶה.
Unique in rulership, properly powerful, His wise ones say to Him, "Yours and Yours, Yours since it is Yours, Yours and even Yours, Yours, Lord is the kingdom; since for Him it is pleasant, for Him it is suited."	יָחִיד בִּמְלוּכָה, כַּבִּיר כַּהֲלָכָה לִמּוּדָיו יֹאמְרוּ לוֹ: לְךָ וּלְךָ, לְךָ כִּי לְךָ, לְךָ אַף לְךָ, לְךָ ה' הַמַּמְלָכָה, כִּי לוֹ נָאֶה, כִּי לוֹ יָאֶה.
Reigning in rulership, properly awesome, those around Him say to Him, "Yours and Yours, Yours since it is Yours, Yours and even Yours, Yours, Lord is the kingdom; since for Him it is pleasant, for Him it is suited."	מוֹשֵׁל בִּמְלוּכָה, נוֹרָא כַּהֲלָכָה סְבִיבָיו יֹאמְרוּ לוֹ: לְךָ וּלְךָ, לְךָ כִּי לְךָ, לְךָ אַף לְךָ, לְךָ ה' הַמַּמְלָכָה, כִּי לוֹ נָאֶה, כִּי לוֹ יָאֶה.
Humble in rulership, properly restoring, His righteous ones say to Him, "Yours and Yours, Yours since it is Yours, Yours and even Yours, Yours, Lord is the kingdom; since for Him it is pleasant, for Him it is suited."	עָנָיו בִּמְלוּכָה, פּוֹדֶה כַּהֲלָכָה, צַדִּיקָיו יֹאמְרוּ לוֹ: לְךָ וּלְךָ, לְךָ כִּי לְךָ, לְךָ אַף לְךָ, לְךָ ה' הַמַּמְלָכָה, כִּי לוֹ נָאֶה, כִּי לוֹ יָאֶה.
Holy in rulership, properly merciful, His angels say to Him, "Yours and Yours, Yours since it is Yours, Yours and even Yours, Yours, Lord is the kingdom; since for Him it is pleasant, for Him it is suited."	קָדוֹשׁ בִּמְלוּכָה, רַחוּם כַּהֲלָכָה שִׁנְאַנָּיו יֹאמְרוּ לוֹ: לְךָ וּלְךָ, לְךָ כִּי לְךָ, לְךָ אַף לְךָ, לְךָ ה' הַמַּמְלָכָה, כִּי לוֹ נָאֶה, כִּי לוֹ יָאֶה.
Dynamic in rulership, properly supportive, His innocent ones say to Him, "Yours and Yours, Yours since it is Yours, Yours and even Yours, Yours, Lord is the kingdom; since for Him it is pleasant, for Him it is suited."	תַּקִּיף בִּמְלוּכָה, תּוֹמֵךְ כַּהֲלָכָה תְּמִימָיו יֹאמְרוּ לוֹ: לְךָ וּלְךָ, לְךָ כִּי לְךָ, לְךָ אַף לְךָ, לְךָ ה' הַמַּמְלָכָה, כִּי לוֹ נָאֶה, כִּי לוֹ יָאֶה.

Mighty is He, may He build His house soon. Quickly, quickly, in our days, soon. God build, God build, build Your house soon.

Chosen is He, great is He, noted is He. Quickly, quickly, in our days, soon. God build, God build, build Your house soon.

Splendid is He, distinguished is He, meritorious is He. Quickly, quickly, in our days, soon. God build, God build, build Your house soon.

Pious is He, pure is He, unique is He. Quickly, quickly, in our days, soon. God build, God build, build Your house soon.

Powerful is He, wise is He, A king is He. Quickly, quickly, in our days, soon. God build, God build, build Your house soon.

Awesome is He, exalted is He, heroic is He. Quickly, quickly, in our days, soon. God build, God build, build Your house soon.

אַדִּיר הוּא יִבְנֶה בֵּיתוֹ בְּקָרוֹב. בִּמְהֵרָה, בִּמְהֵרָה, בְּיָמֵינוּ בְּקָרוֹב. אֵל בְּנֵה, אֵל בְּנֵה, בְּנֵה בֵיתְךָ בְּקָרוֹב.

בָּחוּר הוּא, גָּדוֹל הוּא, דָּגוּל הוּא יִבְנֶה בֵּיתוֹ בְּקָרוֹב. בִּמְהֵרָה, בִּמְהֵרָה, בְּיָמֵינוּ בְּקָרוֹב. אֵל בְּנֵה, אֵל בְּנֵה, בְּנֵה בֵיתְךָ בְּקָרוֹב.

הָדוּר הוּא, וָתִיק הוּא, זַכַּאי הוּא יִבְנֶה בֵּיתוֹ בְּקָרוֹב. בִּמְהֵרָה, בְּיָמֵינוּ בְּקָרוֹב. אֵל בְּנֵה, אֵל בְּנֵה, בְּנֵה בֵיתְךָ בְּקָרוֹב.

חָסִיד הוּא, טָהוֹר הוּא, יָחִיד הוּא יִבְנֶה בֵּיתוֹ בְּקָרוֹב. בִּמְהֵרָה, בִּמְהֵרָה, בְּיָמֵינוּ בְּקָרוֹב. אֵל בְּנֵה, אֵל בְּנֵה, בְּנֵה בֵיתְךָ בְּקָרוֹב.

כַּבִּיר הוּא, לָמוּד הוּא, מֶלֶךְ הוּא יִבְנֶה בֵּיתוֹ בְּקָרוֹב. בִּמְהֵרָה, בִּמְהֵרָה, בְּיָמֵינוּ בְּקָרוֹב. אֵל בְּנֵה, אֵל בְּנֵה, בְּנֵה בֵיתְךָ בְּקָרוֹב.

נוֹרָא הוּא, סַגִּיב הוּא, עִזּוּז הוּא יִבְנֶה בֵּיתוֹ בְּקָרוֹב. בִּמְהֵרָה, בִּמְהֵרָה, בְּיָמֵינוּ בְּקָרוֹב. אֵל בְּנֵה, אֵל בְּנֵה, בְּנֵה בֵיתְךָ בְּקָרוֹב.

A restorer is He, righteous is He, holy is He. Quickly, quickly, in our days, soon. God build, God build, build Your house soon.

Merciful is He, the Omnipotent is He, dynamic is He. Quickly, quickly, in our days, soon. God build, God build, build Your house soon.

פּוֹדֶה הוּא, צַדִּיק הוּא, קָדוֹשׁ הוּא יִבְנֶה בֵּיתוֹ בְּקָרוֹב. בִּמְהֵרָה, בִּמְהֵרָה, בְּיָמֵינוּ בְּקָרוֹב. אֵל בְּנֵה, אֵל בְּנֵה, בְּנֵה בֵיתְךָ בְּקָרוֹב.

רַחוּם הוּא, שַׁדַּי הוּא, תַּקִּיף הוּא יִבְנֶה בֵּיתוֹ בְּקָרוֹב. בִּמְהֵרָה, בִּמְהֵרָה, בְּיָמֵינוּ בְּקָרוֹב. אֵל בְּנֵה, אֵל בְּנֵה, בְּנֵה בֵיתְךָ בְּקָרוֹב.

Sefirat HaOmer

ספירת העומר

The counting of the omer outside of Israel on the second night of Pesach:

ספירת העמר בחוץ לארץ, בליל שני של פסח:

Blessed are You, Lord our God, King of the Universe, who has sanctified us with His commandments and has commanded us on the counting of the omer. Today is the first day of the omer.

בָּרוּךְ אַתָּה ה', אֱלֹהֵינוּ מֶלֶךְ הָעוֹלָם, אֲשֶׁר קִדְּשָׁנוּ בְּמִצְוֹתָיו וְצִוָּנוּ עַל סְפִירַת הָעֹמֶר. הַיּוֹם יוֹם אֶחָד בָּעֹמֶר.

Echad Mi Yodea

Who knows one? I know one: One is our God in the heavens and the earth.

אחד מי יודע

אֶחָד מִי יוֹדֵעַ? אֶחָד אֲנִי יוֹדֵעַ: אֶחָד אֱלֹהֵינוּ שֶׁבַּשָּׁמַיִם וּבָאָרֶץ.

I KNOW!

Who knows two? I know two: two are the tablets of the covenant, One is our God in the heavens and the earth.

שְׁנַיִם מִי יוֹדֵעַ? שְׁנַיִם אֲנִי יוֹדֵעַ: שְׁנֵי לֻחוֹת הַבְּרִית. אֶחָד אֱלֹהֵינוּ שֶׁבַּשָּׁמַיִם וּבָאָרֶץ.

S5E14: The One Where Everybody Finds Out
Phoebe discovers Chandler and Monica's secret relationship through Ugly Naked Guy's apartment window:
Phoebe: (looking out the window) Oh, look! There's Monica and Chandler! (Starts yelling.) Hey! Hey, you guys! Hey! Ohh!! Ohh! Ahh-ahhh!!
Rachel: What?!
Phoebe: (screaming) Ahhh!! Chandler and Monica!! Chandler and Monica!!
Rachel: Oh my God!
Phoebe: CHANDLER AND MONICA!!!!
Rachel: OH MY GOD!!!
Phoebe: OH!! MY EYES!!! MY EYES!!!!
Rachel: Phoebe!! Phoebe!! It's okay!! It's okay!!
Phoebe: NO! THEY'RE DOING IT!!!
Rachel: I KNOW!! I KNOW!! I KNOW!
Phoebe: YOU KNOW?!!!
Rachel: Yes, I know! And Joey knows! But Ross doesn't know so you have to stop screaming!!

....

Rachel: Joey, do they know that we know?
Joey: No.
Rachel: Joey!
Joey: They know you know.
Rachel: Ugh, I knew it! Oh I cannot believe those **TWO**!
Phoebe: God, they thought they can mess with us! They're trying to mess with us?! They don't know that we know they know we know! (Joey just shakes his head.) Joey, you can't say anything!
Joey: I couldn't even if I wanted to.

THEY DON'T KNOW THAT WE KNOW THEY KNOW WE KNOW!

Who knows three? I know three: three are the fathers, two are the tablets of the covenant, One is our God in the heavens and the earth.

שְׁלֹשָׁה מִי יוֹדֵעַ? שְׁלֹשָׁה אֲנִי יוֹדֵעַ:
שְׁלֹשָׁה אָבוֹת, שְׁנֵי לֻחוֹת הַבְּרִית,
אֶחָד אֱלֹהֵינוּ שֶׁבַּשָּׁמַיִם וּבָאָרֶץ.

S2E4: The One with Phoebe's Husband
Chandler: I didn't know it was a big secret.
Monica: Oh it's not big, not at all, you know, kinda the same lines as, say, oh i don't know, having a **third nipple**.
Phoebe: You have a third nipple?
Chandler: You b*tch.
Ross: Whip it out, whip it out.
Chandler: C'mon, there's nothin' to see, it's just a tiny bump, it's totally useless.
Rachel: Oh as, as opposed to your other multi-functional nipples?
Joey: I can't believe you. You told me it was a nubbin.
Ross: Joey, what did you think a nubbin was?
Joey: I don't know, you see somethin', you hear a word, i thought that's what it was. Let me see it again.
All: Yeah, show it. Show it. The nubbin, the nubbin, the nubbin.
Ross: [to chandler] So what's it shaped like?
Phoebe: Yeah, is there a hair on it?
Joey: What happens if you flick it?

....

[Chandler, ross, and julie are sitting on the couch in Central Perk.]
Ross: So, uh, does it do anything, you know, special?
Chandler: Why yes ross, pressing my third nipple opens the delivery entrance to the magical land of narnia.
Julie: You know, in some cultures having a third nipple is actually a sign of virility. You get the best huts and women dance naked around you.
Chandler: Huh? Are, uh, any of these cultures, per chance, in the tri-state area?

Who knows four? I know four: four are the mothers, three are the fathers, two are the tablets of the covenant, One is our God in the heavens and the earth.

אַרְבַּע מִי יוֹדֵעַ? אַרְבַּע אֲנִי יוֹדֵעַ: אַרְבַּע אִמָּהוֹת, שְׁלשָׁה אָבוֹת, שְׁנֵי לֻחוֹת הַבְּרִית, אֶחָד אֱלֹהֵינוּ שֶׁבַּשָּׁמַיִם וּבָאָרֶץ.

Rachels's 4 Jobs

86 — Waitress at Central Perk

87 — Assistant at Fortunata Fashions

88 — Buyer and personal shopper at Bloomingdale's

89 — Executive at Ralph Lauren

Who knows five? I know five: five are the books of the Torah, four are the mothers, three are the fathers, two are the tablets of the covenant, One is our God in the heavens and the earth.

חֲמִשָּׁה מִי יוֹדֵעַ? חֲמִשָּׁה אֲנִי יוֹדֵעַ: חֲמִשָּׁה חֻמְשֵׁי תוֹרָה, אַרְבַּע אִמָּהוֹת, שְׁלשָׁה אָבוֹת, שְׁנֵי לֻחוֹת הַבְּרִית, אֶחָד אֱלֹהֵינוּ שֶׁבַּשָּׁמַיִם וּבָאָרֶץ.

Five is the number of "friends" who have lived in Monica's apartment at one point during the show.

Who knows six? I know six: six are the orders of the Mishnah, five are the books of the Torah, four are the mothers, three are the fathers, two are the tablets of the covenant, One is our God in the heavens and the earth.

שִׁשָּׁה מִי יוֹדֵעַ? שִׁשָּׁה אֲנִי יוֹדֵעַ: שִׁשָּׁה סִדְרֵי מִשְׁנָה, חֲמִשָּׁה חוּמְשֵׁי תוֹרָה, אַרְבַּע אִמָּהוֹת, שְׁלֹשָׁה אָבוֹת, שְׁנֵי לֻחוֹת הַבְּרִית, אֶחָד אֱלֹהֵינוּ שֶׁבַּשָּׁמַיִם וּבָאָרֶץ.

6 Friends Forever

Who knows seven? I know seven: seven are the days of the week, six are the orders of the Mishnah, five are the books of the Torah, four are the mothers, three are the fathers, two are the tablets of the covenant, One is our God in the heavens and the earth.

שִׁבְעָה מִי יוֹדֵעַ? שִׁבְעָה אֲנִי יוֹדֵעַ: שִׁבְעָה יְמֵי שַׁבַּתָּא, שִׁשָּׁה סִדְרֵי מִשְׁנָה, חֲמִשָּׁה חוּמְשֵׁי תּוֹרָה, אַרְבַּע אִמָּהוֹת, שְׁלֹשָׁה אָבוֹת, שְׁנֵי לֻחוֹת הַבְּרִית, אֶחָד אֱלֹהֵינוּ שֶׁבַּשָּׁמַיִם וּבָאָרֶץ.

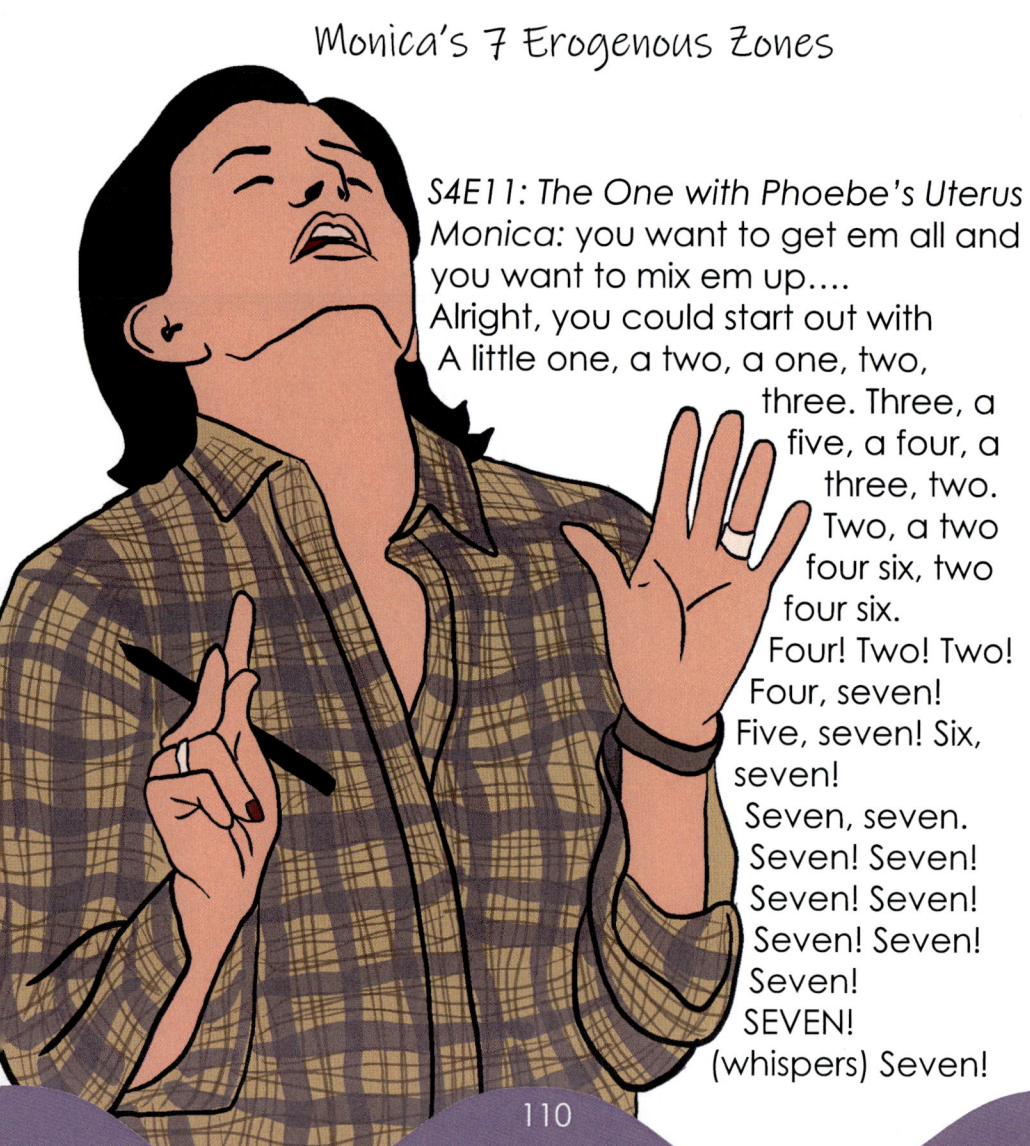

Monica's 7 Erogenous Zones

S4E11: The One with Phoebe's Uterus
Monica: you want to get em all and you want to mix em up....
Alright, you could start out with A little one, a two, a one, two, three. Three, a five, a four, a three, two. Two, a two four six, two four six. Four! Two! Two! Four, seven! Five, seven! Six, seven! Seven, seven. Seven! Seven! Seven! Seven! Seven! Seven! Seven! SEVEN! (whispers) Seven!

Who knows eight? I know eight: eight are the days of circumcision, seven are the days of the week, six are the orders of the Mishnah, five are the books of the Torah, four are the mothers, three are the fathers, two are the tablets of the covenant, One is our God in the heavens and the earth.

שְׁמוֹנָה מִי יוֹדֵעַ? שְׁמוֹנָה אֲנִי יוֹדֵעַ: שְׁמוֹנָה יְמֵי מִילָה, שִׁבְעָה יְמֵי שַׁבָּתָא, שִׁשָּׁה סִדְרֵי מִשְׁנָה, חֲמִשָּׁה חוּמְשֵׁי תוֹרָה, אַרְבַּע אִמָּהוֹת, שְׁלֹשָׁה אָבוֹת, שְׁנֵי לֻחוֹת הַבְּרִית, אֶחָד אֱלֹהֵינוּ שֶׁבַּשָּׁמַיִם וּבָאָרֶץ.

8 Shades of Ross's Tan

Who knows nine? I know nine: nine are the months of birth, eight are the days of circumcision, seven are the days of the week, six are the orders of the Mishnah, five are the books of the Torah, four are the mothers, three are the fathers, two are the tablets of the covenant, One is our God in the heavens and the earth.

תִּשְׁעָה מִי יוֹדֵעַ? תִּשְׁעָה אֲנִי יוֹדֵעַ: תִּשְׁעָה יַרְחֵי לֵדָה, שְׁמוֹנָה יְמֵי מִילָה, שִׁבְעָה יְמֵי שַׁבָּתָא, שִׁשָּׁה סִדְרֵי מִשְׁנָה, חֲמִשָּׁה חוּמְשֵׁי תוֹרָה, אַרְבַּע אִמָּהוֹת, שְׁלֹשָׁה אָבוֹת, שְׁנֵי לֻחוֹת הַבְּרִית, אֶחָד אֱלֹהֵינוּ שֶׁבַּשָּׁמַיִם וּבָאָרֶץ.

9 of Chandler's Remaining Toes[91]

Who knows ten? I know ten: ten are the statements, nine are the months of birth, eight are the days of circumcision, seven are the days of the week, six are the orders of the Mishnah, five are the books of the Torah, four are the mothers, three are the fathers, two are the tablets of the covenant, One is our God in the heavens and the earth.

עֲשָׂרָה מִי יוֹדֵעַ? עֲשָׂרָה אֲנִי יוֹדֵעַ: עֲשָׂרָה דִבְּרַיָּא, תִּשְׁעָה יַרְחֵי לֵדָה, שְׁמוֹנָה יְמֵי מִילָה, שִׁבְעָה יְמֵי שַׁבַּתָּא, שִׁשָּׁה סִדְרֵי מִשְׁנָה, חֲמִשָּׁה חוּמְשֵׁי תוֹרָה, אַרְבַּע אִמָּהוֹת, שְׁלשָׁה אָבוֹת, שְׁנֵי לֻחוֹת הַבְּרִית, אֶחָד אֱלֹהֵינוּ שֶׁבַּשָּׁמַיִם וּבָאָרֶץ.

10 Fantastic Seasons of FRIENDS

Who knows eleven? I know eleven: eleven are the stars, ten are the statements, nine are the months of birth, eight are the days of circumcision, seven are the days of the week, six are the orders of the Mishnah, five are the books of the Torah, four are the mothers, three are the fathers, two are the tablets of the covenant, One is our God in the heavens and the earth.

עֲשָׂרָה אַחַד עָשָׂר מִי יוֹדֵעַ? אַחַד עָשָׂר אֲנִי יוֹדֵעַ: אַחַד עָשָׂר כּוֹכְבַיָּא, עֲשָׂרָה דִבְּרַיָּא, תִּשְׁעָה יַרְחֵי לֵדָה, שְׁמוֹנָה יְמֵי מִילָה, שִׁבְעָה יְמֵי שַׁבַּתָּא, שִׁשָּׁה סִדְרֵי מִשְׁנָה, חֲמִשָּׁה חוּמְשֵׁי תוֹרָה, אַרְבַּע אִמָּהוֹת, שְׁלשָׁה אָבוֹת, שְׁנֵי לֻחוֹת הַבְּרִית, אֶחָד אֱלֹהֵינוּ שֶׁבַּשָּׁמַיִם וּבָאָרֶץ.

11 Categories of Monica's Towels[92]

1. Guest
2. Fancy guest
3. Personal
4. Fancy personal
5. Decorative bathroom (not to be used)
6. Parents or UBER special guest
7. Cleaning
8. Kitchen (dish towels)
9. Decorative kitchen towels
10. Ones specifically for hair
11. Ones specifically for male "guests"

Who knows twelve? I know twelve: twelve are the tribes, eleven are the stars, ten are the statements, nine are the months of birth, eight are the days of circumcision, seven are the days of the week, six are the orders of the Mishnah, five are the books of the Torah, four are the mothers, three are the fathers, two are the tablets of the covenant, One is our God in the heavens and the earth.

שְׁנֵים עָשָׂר מִי יוֹדֵעַ? שְׁנֵים עָשָׂר אֲנִי יוֹדֵעַ: שְׁנֵים עָשָׂר שִׁבְטַיָּא, אַחַד עָשָׂר כּוֹכְבַיָּא, עֲשָׂרָה דִבְּרַיָּא, תִּשְׁעָה יַרְחֵי לֵדָה, שְׁמוֹנָה יְמֵי מִילָה, שִׁבְעָה יְמֵי שַׁבַּתָּא, שִׁשָּׁה סִדְרֵי מִשְׁנָה, חֲמִשָּׁה חוּמְשֵׁי תוֹרָה, אַרְבַּע אִמָּהוֹת, שְׁלֹשָׁה אָבוֹת, שְׁנֵי לֻחוֹת הַבְּרִית, אֶחָד אֱלֹהֵינוּ שֶׁבַּשָּׁמַיִם וּבָאָרֶץ.

The meat's only every third layer... maybe you can scrape?[93]

12 Lasagnas Monica made for her Aunt Syl (which were not vegetarian)

Who knows thirteen? I know thirteen: thirteen are the characteristics, twelve are the tribes, eleven are the stars, ten are the statements, nine are the months of birth, eight are the days of circumcision, seven are the days of the week, six are the orders of the Mishnah, five are the books of the Torah, four are the mothers, three are the fathers, two are the tablets of the covenant, One is our God in the heavens and the earth.

שְׁלֹשָׁה עָשָׂר מִי יוֹדֵעַ? שְׁלֹשָׁה עָשָׂר אֲנִי יוֹדֵעַ: שְׁלֹשָׁה עָשָׂר מִדַּיָּא. שְׁנֵים עָשָׂר שִׁבְטַיָּא, אַחַד עָשָׂר כּוֹכְבַיָּא, עֲשָׂרָה דִבְּרַיָּא, תִּשְׁעָה יַרְחֵי לֵדָה, שְׁמוֹנָה יְמֵי מִילָה, שִׁבְעָה יְמֵי שַׁבַּתָּא, שִׁשָּׁה סִדְרֵי מִשְׁנָה, חֲמִשָּׁה חוּמְשֵׁי תוֹרָה, אַרְבַּע אִמָּהוֹת, שְׁלֹשָׁה אָבוֹת, שְׁנֵי לֻחוֹת הַבְּרִית, אֶחָד אֱלֹהֵינוּ שֶׁבַּשָּׁמַיִם וּבָאָרֶץ.

13: The Age at which Monica Learned How to Tell Time[94]

Chad Gadya

One kid, one kid that my father bought for two zuz, one kid, one kid.

Then came a cat and ate the kid that my father bought for two zuz, one kid, one kid.

Then came a dog and bit the cat, that ate the kid that my father bought for two zuz, one kid, one kid.

Then came a stick and hit the dog, that bit the cat, that ate the kid that my father bought for two zuz, one kid, one kid.

Then came fire and burnt the stick, that hit the dog, that bit the cat, that ate the kid that my father bought for two zuz, one kid, one kid.

Then came water and extinguished the fire, that burnt the stick, that hit the dog, that bit the cat, that ate the kid that my father bought for two zuz, one kid, one kid.

Then came a bull and drank the water, that extinguished the fire, that burnt the stick, that hit the dog, that bit the cat, that ate the kid that my father bought for two zuz, one kid, one kid.

חד גדיא

חַד גַּדְיָא, חַד גַּדְיָא דְזַבִּין אַבָּא בִּתְרֵי זוּזֵי, חַד גַּדְיָא, חַד גַּדְיָא.

וְאָתָא שׁוּנְרָא וְאָכְלָה לְגַדְיָא, דְזַבִּין אַבָּא בִּתְרֵי זוּזֵי. חַד גַּדְיָא, חַד גַּדְיָא.

וְאָתָא כַלְבָּא וְנָשַׁךְ לְשׁוּנְרָא, דְאָכְלָה לְגַדְיָא, דְזַבִּין אַבָּא בִּתְרֵי זוּזֵי. חַד גַּדְיָא, חַד גַּדְיָא.

וְאָתָא חוּטְרָא וְהִכָּה לְכַלְבָּא, דְנָשַׁךְ לְשׁוּנְרָא, דְאָכְלָה לְגַדְיָא, דְזַבִּין אַבָּא בִּתְרֵי זוּזֵי. חַד גַּדְיָא, חַד גַּדְיָא.

וְאָתָא נוּרָא וְשָׂרַף לְחוּטְרָא, דְהִכָּה לְכַלְבָּא, דְנָשַׁךְ לְשׁוּנְרָא, דְאָכְלָה לְגַדְיָא, דְזַבִּין אַבָּא בִּתְרֵי זוּזֵי. חַד גַּדְיָא, חַד גַּדְיָא.

וְאָתָא מַיָּא וְכָבָה לְנוּרָא, דְשָׂרַף לְחוּטְרָא, דְהִכָּה לְכַלְבָּא, דְנָשַׁךְ לְשׁוּנְרָא, דְאָכְלָה לְגַדְיָא, דְזַבִּין אַבָּא בִּתְרֵי זוּזֵי. חַד גַּדְיָא, חַד גַּדְיָא.

וְאָתָא תוֹרָא וְשָׁתָה לְמַיָּא, דְכָבָה לְנוּרָא, דְשָׂרַף לְחוּטְרָא, דְהִכָּה לְכַלְבָּא, דְנָשַׁךְ לְשׁוּנְרָא, דְאָכְלָה לְגַדְיָא, דְזַבִּין אַבָּא בִּתְרֵי זוּזֵי. חַד גַּדְיָא, חַד גַּדְיָא.

Then came the schochet and slaughtered the bull, that drank the water, that extinguished the fire, that burnt the stick, that hit the dog, that bit the cat, that ate the kid that my father bought for two zuz, one kid, one kid.

וְאָתָא הַשׁוֹחֵט וְשָׁחַט לְתוֹרָא, דְּשָׁתָה לְמַיָּא, דְּכָבָה לְנוּרָא, דְּשָׂרַף לְחוּטְרָא, דְּהִכָּה לְכַלְבָּא, דְּנָשַׁךְ לְשׁוּנְרָא, דְּאָכְלָה לְגַדְיָא, דְּזַבִּין אַבָּא בִּתְרֵי זוּזֵי. חַד גַּדְיָא, חַד גַּדְיָא.

Then came the angel of death and slaughtered the schochet, who slaughtered the bull, that drank the water, that extinguished the fire, that burnt the stick, that hit the dog, that bit the cat, that ate the kid that my father bought for two zuz, one kid, one kid.

וְאָתָא מַלְאַךְ הַמָּוֶת וְשָׁחַט לְשׁוֹחֵט, דְּשָׁחַט לְתוֹרָא, דְּשָׁתָה לְמַיָּא, דְּכָבָה לְנוּרָא, דְּשָׂרַף לְחוּטְרָא, דְּהִכָּה לְכַלְבָּא, דְּנָשַׁךְ לְשׁוּנְרָא, דְּאָכְלָה לְגַדְיָא, דְּזַבִּין אַבָּא בִּתְרֵי זוּזֵי. חַד גַּדְיָא, חַד גַּדְיָא.

Then came the Holy One, blessed be He and slaughtered the angel of death, who slaughtered the schochet, who slaughtered the bull, that drank the water, that extinguished the fire, that burnt the stick, that hit the dog, that bit the cat, that ate the kid that my father bought for two zuz, one kid, one kid.

וְאָתָא הַקָּדוֹשׁ בָּרוּךְ הוּא וְשָׁחַט לְמַלְאַךְ הַמָּוֶת, דְּשָׁחַט לְשׁוֹחֵט, דְּשָׁחַט לְתוֹרָא, דְּשָׁתָה לְמַיָּא, דְּכָבָה לְנוּרָא, דְּשָׂרַף לְחוּטְרָא, דְּהִכָּה לְכַלְבָּא, דְּנָשַׁךְ לְשׁוּנְרָא, דְּאָכְלָה לְגַדְיָא, דְּזַבִּין אַבָּא בִּתְרֵי זוּזֵי. חַד גַּדְיָא, חַד גַּדְיָא.

PHOEBE'S JINGLES

CENTRAL PERK

PRESENTS

MISS PHOEBE BUFFAY

S1E1: The One Where Monica Gets A New Roommate

A FEW OF MY FAVORITE THINGS

Raindrops on roses
and rabbits and kittens
Bluebells and sleigh bells
and something with mittens
la la la la la la
something with string....

LOVE

Love is sweet as summer showers,
Love is a wondrous work of art,
But your love oh your love,
your love...
Is like a giant pigeon...
crapping on my heart.
La-la-la-la-la-
(some guy gives her some change
and to that guy she says)
Thank you.
La-la-la-la...ohhh!

S1E7: The One With The Blackout

Blackout
New York City has no power
And the milk is getting sour
But to me that is not scary
Cause I stay away from dairy
La-la-la-la-la-la...

S1E10: The One With The Monkey

Cremated

My mother's ashes
Even her eyelashes
Are resting in a little yellow jar

and sometimes when it's breezy
Or if i'm feeling sneezy
And now I......

S1E10: The One With The Monkey

Snowman

I made a man with eyes of coal
and a smile so bewitchin'
How was I supposed to know that my mom was dead in the kitchen
La-la-la-la-la...

S1E11: TOW Mrs. Bing

My Coma Guy

You don't have to be awake to be my man
As long as you have brain waves
I'll be there to hold your hand.
Though we just met the other day
There's something I have got to say...

S1E23: The One With The Birth

WAAA!

Babies
They're tiny and chubby
and so sweet to touch
Soon they'll grow up
and resent you so much
Now they're yelling at
you and you don't
know why
And you cry and you
cry and you cry
And you cry and you cry...

Trapped in the Hospital Closet
And they found their bodies the very next day,
they found their bodies the very next day,
la la la, la la la, la la la...

S2E6: The One With The Baby On The Bus

Double-Jointed Boy
He was a double, double, double-jointed boy

S2E6: The One With The Baby On The Bus

In the Shower

I'm in the shower and I'm writing a song. Stop me if you've heard it.

My skin is soapy, and my hair is wet, and Tegrin spelled backward is Nirget. Lather, rinse, repeat and lather, rinse, repeat and lather, rinse, repeat as needed.

Stephanie

Stephanie knows all the chords!

S2E6: The One With The Baby On The Bus

When I Play
When I play, I play for me
I don't need your charity
La lalala lalalalalala
lalala lalala lalalalalala....

Terry's a Jerk
Terry's a jerk!
And he won't let me work!
And I hate Central Perk!
And you're all invited
to bite me!

S2E8: The One With The List

Two of Them Kissed Last Night

There was a girl we'll call her Betty
And a guy let's call him Neil
Now I can't stress this point too strongly
This story isn't real.
Now our Neil must decide
Who will be the girl that he casts aside?
Will Betty be the one who he loves truly
Or will it be the one who we'll call L-L-Loolie?
He must decide, he must decide
Even though I made him up he must decide

MOO

S2E12: The One After The Superbowl

Barnyard Animals

Oh the cow in the meadow goes "moo"
Oh the cow in the meadow goes "moo"
Then the farmer hits him on the head
and grinds him up
And that's how we get hamburgers.
Noooowwwww chickens!

Don't

There'll be times when you get older
And you'll want to sleep with people
Just to make them like you
But DON'T
Cause that's another thing that you don't wanna do
That's another thing that you don't wanna do

Bi-sexuals

Sometimes men love women
And sometimes men love men
Then there are bi-sexuals
Though some just say they're kidding themselves
La-la-la-la-la-la...

Grandma

Now grandma's a person who everyone likes
She brought you a train and a bright shiny bike
But lately she hasn't been coming to dinner
And last time you saw her she looked so much thinner.
Now your mom and your dad said she moved to Peru,
But the truth is she died and someday you will too
La-la-la-la-la...

S2E18: The One Where Dr. Ramoray Dies

Crusty Old Man
And the crusty old man said "I'll do what I can"
And the rest of the rats played maracas

S3E14: TOW Phoebe's Ex-Partner

Jingle B*tch
Jingle b*tch screwed me over
Go to hell jingle wh*re
Go to hell, go to hell, go to h-h-hell

Sticky Shoes
My favorite shoes, so good to me,
I wear them everyday.
Down at the heel, holes in the toes,
don't care what people say.
My feet's best friends, pals to the end, with them
I'm one hot chicky.
Though late one night, not much light,
I stepped in something icky.
Sticky shoes, sticky shoes,
always make me smile.
Sticky shoes, sticky shoes,
next time I'll avoid
the pile!

S4E1: The One With The Jellyfish

THE 66 COLORS OF MY BEDROOM

...and

FUSCHIA AND MAUVE

Those are the
66 COLORS
of my bedroom.

S3E23: The One With Ross' Thing

Crazy Underwear
Crazy underwear
creeping up my butt
Crazy underwear
always in a rut
Crazy underwear...

S4E2: The One With The Cat

Dumb Drunken B*tch
...dumb. Drunken. b*tch!!!

S4E5: The One With Joey's New Girlfriend

Parading Goats
Parading goats are parading,
Parading down the street.
Parading goats are parading,
Leaving little treats!

Paper Maché
(three snaps)
I, I'm still waiting
for my paper maché man

S4E7: The One Where Chandler Crosses The Line

Tony Tarzan
Little Tony Tarzan
Swinging on
a nose hair
Swinging with the
greatest of
ease...

S4E10: The One With The Girl From Poughkeepsie

HOLIDAY SONG

Went to the store, sat on Santa's lap
Asked him to bring my friends all kinds of crap
Said all you need is to write them a song
Now you haven't heard it yet so don't try to sing along
No don't sing along...
Monica, Monica, have a Happy Hanukkah!
Saw Santa Claus, he said hello to Ross
And please tell Joey, Christmas will be snowwwwwy
And Rachel and Chandler,
Ha ah ha ah handler!

S6E3: The One With Ross' Denial

Ode To a Pubic Hair
I found you in my bed!
How'd you wind up there?
You are a mystery,
Little black curly hair!
  Little black curly hair!
    Little black,
      little black,
        Little black,
         little black,
Little-Black-Curly-Hair

S6E16: The One That Could've Been Part II

Two Heart Attacks
It only takes two
heart attacks
to finally make
you see
one of them
won't do it
but the second will
set you free
Tell all your hate and anger
it's time to say good bye
and that is just what I will do
as soon as those bastards
I work for die
Lalalalalalalalalala...

S4E12: The One With The Embryos

Little Fetus
Are you in there little fetus?
In nine months will you come greet us?
I will...buy you some Adidas.

S7E1: TOW Monica's Thunder

First Time I Met Chandler
The first time I met Chandler
I thought he was gay
but here I am singing
on his wedding daaaay

Whenever I Get Married
Whenever I get married
Guess who won't be asked to sing?
Somebody named Geller!
And somebody else named Bing!!!

Who will perform the Ceremony
Who will perform the ceremony?
Who will perform the ceremony?

She Just Stayed and Stayed
We thought Phoebe would leave
But she just stayed and stayed
That's right, here all night
And Chandler will never get Lai...

S9E19: The One With Rachel's Dream

Argentina Song
And there's a country
called Argentina
It's a place
I've never seen
But I'm told for
fifty pesos
You can buy a human
spleeeeen
Human
spleen!
Olé!

The Woman Smelled Like Garbage
It wasn't just that she was fat,
The woman smelled like garbage!
Everyone!
It wasn't just that she was fat,
The woman smelled like gaaaarbage!
Classy huh?

The Food Here At Javu
The food here at
Javu...will kill you!
The food here at
Javu...will kill you!

S10E4: The One With The Cake
Emma's Bithday Song
Emma,
Your name poses a dilemna,
'Cause not much else rhymes with Emma.
Maybe the actor Richard Crenna
(he played the commanding officer in Rambo)
Happy Birthday Emma!

S10E17 & 18: The Last One

Best Day Ever
Aahh, aahh, aahh...
When the sun comes up,
bright and beaming!
And the moon comes...

Don't Take No
Bum bum bum
Don't take no for an answer!
Bum bum bum
Don't let love fly away!
Bum bum bum bum bum bum...

S2E17: The One Where Eddie Moves In

Smelly Cat
Smelly cat, smelly cat
What are they feeding you?
Smelly cat, smelly cat
It's not your fault
They won't take you to the vet
        You're obviously not
           their favorite pet
        You may not be
        a bed of roses
           And you're no friend to
              those with noses

The Seder is Concluded...

S4E1: The One With The Jellyfish
Ross: Done!
Rachel: You just finished?
Ross: Well I wanted to be thorough, I mean this is clearly very very important to you, to us. And so I wanted to read every word, carefully…twice!

S4E1: The One With The Jellyfish
Ross: I didn't finish the letter!
Rachel: What?
Ross: I fell asleep
Rachel: you fell asleep???

It was 5:30 in the morning, and you had rambled on for 18 pages...

FRONT AND BACK!

96

Monica: What are you doing?
Joey: I think I left a donut up here.[97]

47 *S3E25: THE ONE AT THE BEACH*
48 *S3E3: TOW THE JAM*
49 *S10E8: TOW THE LATE THANKSGIVING*
50 *S4E3: TOW THE 'CUFFS*
51 *S3E2: THE ONE WHERE NO ONE IS READY*
52 *S7E8: TOW CHANDLER DOESN'T LIKE DOGS*
53 *S4E7: TOW CHANDLER CROSSES THE LINE*
54 *S2E2: TOW THE BREAST MILK*
55 *S5E9: TOW ROSS'S SANDWICH*
56 *S5E9: TOW ROSS'S SANDWICH*
57 *S5E9: TOW ROSS'S SANDWICH*
58 *S5E9: TOW ROSS'S SANDWICH*
59 *S10E8: TOW THE LATE THANKSGIVING*
60 *S6E17: TOW UNAGI*
61 *S2E20: TOW OLD YELLER DIES*
62 *S1E2: TOW THE SONOGRAM AT THE END*
63 *S8E12 TOW JOEY DATES RACHEL*
64 *S10E8: TOW THE LATE THANKSGIVING*
65 *S2E24: TOW BARRY AND MINDY'S WEDDING*
66 *S8E23: TOW RACHEL HAS A BABY*
67 *S7E7: TOW ROSS'S LIBRARY BOOK*
68 *S4E15: TOW ALL THE RUGBY*
69 *S10E15: TOW ESTELLE DIES*
70 *S1E14: TOW THE CANDY HEARTS*
71 *S7E6: TOW THE NAP PARTNERS*
72 *S4E2: TOW THE CAT*
73 *S10E11: TOW THE STRIPPER CRIES*
74 *S7E23: TOW MONICA AND CHANDLER'S WEDDING*
75 *S5E16: TOW THE COP*
76 *S5E9: TOW ROSS'S SANDWICH*
77 *S9E3: TOW THE PEDIATRICIAN*
78 *S2E1: TOW ROSS'S NEW GIRLFRIEND*
79 *S6E2: TOW ROSS HUGS RACHEL*
80 *S9E11: TOW RACHEL GOES BACK TO WORK*
81 *S5E11: TOW ALL THE RESOLUTIONS*
82 *S5E14: TOW EVERYBODY FINDS OUT*
83 *S5E14: TOW EVERYBODY FINDS OUT*
84 *S5E5: TOW THE KIPS*
85 *S5E14: TOW EVERYBODY FINDS OUT*
86 *S1E22: TOW THE ICK FACTOR*
87 *S3E10: TOW RACHEL QUITS*
88 *S4E13: TOW RACHEL'S CRUSH*
89 *S7E4: TOW RACHEL'S ASSISTANT*
90 *S10E3: TOW ROSS'S TAN*
91 *S5E8: TOW ALL THE THANKSGIVINGS*
92 *S4E12: TOW THE EMBRYOS*
93 *S1E12: TOW THE DOZEN LASAGNAS*
94 *S7E4: TOW RACHEL'S ASSISTANT*
95 *S1E10: TOW THE MONKEY*
96 *S9E22: TOW THE DONOR*
97 *S4E13: TOW RACHEL'S CRUSH*

EPISODE GUIDE

1 *S9E1: TOW THE MALE NANNY*
2 *S1E14: TOW THE CANDY HEARTS*
3 *S3E20: TOW THE DOLLHOUSE*
4 *S6E18: TOW ROSS DATES A STUDENT*
5 *S2E11: TOW THE LESBIAN WEDDING*
6 *S2E21: TOW THE BULLIES*
7 *S5E9: TOW ROSS'S SANDWICH*
8 *S7E8: TOW CHANDLER DOESN'T LIKE DOGS*
9 *S3E3: TOW THE JAM*
10 *S1E9: TOW UNDERDOG GETS AWAY*
11 *S2E8: TOW THE LIST*
12 *S7E3: TOW PHOEBE'S COOKIES*
13 *S6E9: TOW ROSS GOT HIGH*
14 *S7E11: TOW ALL THE CHEESECAKES*
15 *S5E16: TOW THE COP*
16 *S5E8: TOW ALL THE THANKSGIVINGS*
17 *S10E8: TOW THE LATE THANKSGIVING*
18 *S4E12: TOW THE EMBRYOS*
19 *S5E8: TOW ALL THE THANKSGIVINGS*
20 *S4E3: TOW THE 'CUFFS*
21 *S8E6: TOW THE HALLOWEEN PARTY*
22 *S3E2: THE ONE WHERE NO ONE IS READY*
23 *S2E24: TOW BARRY AND MINDY'S WEDDING*
24 *S3E2: THE ONE WHERE NO ONE IS READY*
25 *S8E6: TOW THE HALLOWEEN PARTY*
26 *S3E15: TOW ROSS AND RACHEL TAKE A BREAK*
27 *S10E9: TOW THE BIRTH MOTHER*
28 *S6E3: TOW ROSS'S DENIAL*
29 *S6E12: TOW THE JOKE*
30 *S4E12: TOW THE EMBRYOS*
31 *S4E19: TOW ALL THE HASTE*
32 *S10E2: TOW ROSS IS FINE*
33 *S5E9: TOW ROSS'S SANDWICH*
34 *S7E8: TOW CHANDLER DOESN'T LIKE DOGS*
35 *S9E15: TOW THE MUGGING*
36 *S7E11: TOW ALL THE CHEESECAKES*
37 *S7E14: TOW THEY ALL TURN THIRTY*
38 *S5E6: TOW THE YETI*
39 *S4E12: TOW THE EMBRYOS*
40 *S6E20: TOW MAC AND C.H.E.E.S.E.*
41 *S1E19: TOW THE MONKEY GETS AWAY*
42 *S5E21: TOW THE BALL*
43 *S1E9: TOW UNDERDOG GETS AWAY*
44 *S2E23: TOW THE CHICKEN POX*
45 *S1E21: TOW THE FAKE MONICA*
46 *S7E10: TOW THE HOLIDAY ARMADILLO*

THE ONE WITH THE VERY LONG SEDER

THE UNOFFICIAL *FRIENDS* HAGGADAH

● ● ● ● ● ●

AUTHOR: ROCHEL LEAH MARINELLI
CO-AUTHOR AND ILLUSTRATOR: GAYIL ZEILBERGER

Copyright © 2023 TOW 2 SISTERS LLC
Rochel Leah Marinelli & Gayil Zeilberger
The One With the Very Long Seder:
The Unofficial FRIENDS Haggadah

Illustrations by Gayil Zeilberger
Hebrew text adapted from Sefaria.org

All rights reserved. No portion of this book may be reproduced in any form without permission from the publisher, except as permitted by U.S. copyright law.

FRIENDS transcripts used for parody purposes only
ISBN: 9798366213721
Printed in USA

SO NO ONE TOLD YOU LIFE WAS GONNA BE THIS WAY

YOUR JOB'S A JOKE, YOU'RE BROKE

YOUR LOVE LIFE'S DOA

IT'S LIKE YOU'RE ALWAYS STUCK IN SECOND GEAR

WHEN IT HASN'T BEEN YOUR DAY, YOUR WEEK,

YOUR MONTH OR EVEN YOUR YEAR, BUT

I'LL BE THERE FOR YOU

(WHEN THE RAIN STARTS TO POUR)

I'LL BE THERE FOR YOU

(LIKE I'VE BEEN THERE BEFORE)

I'LL BE THERE FOR YOU

('CAUSE YOU'RE THERE FOR ME TOO)

-THE REMBRANDTS (I'LL BE THERE FOR YOU)